WRITERS REPUBLIC

WAKE THE
MIRROR

VINCENTE TORBOLI

WRITERS REPUBLIC L.L.C.
515 Summit Ave. Unit R1
Union City, NJ 07087, USA

Website: *www.writersrepublic.com*
Hotline: *1-877-656-6838*
Email: *info@writersrepublic.com*

Ordering Information:
Quantity sales. Special discounts are available on quantity purchases by corporations, associations, and others. For details, contact the publisher at the address above.

Library of Congress Control Number:		2023940210
ISBN-13:	979-8-88810-781-2	[Paperback Edition]
	979-8-88810-782-9	[Digital Edition]

Rev. date: 06/22/2023

CONTENTS

WAKE THE MIRROR

There is a place between you and me,
If you listen for the lost, you may hear their screams.

Though their cries are definite, the origin is extraneous.
For the shrieks are the door, and the road simultaneous.

They will beg, they will whimper, your nihilism will ensure.
You won't allow a fairy tale, your reflections too impure.

Over the wailing of departed, we begin to hear ourselves clearer.
If you wish to see yourself again, you must simply wake the mirror.

The Argus Affliction

"I feel like I'm losing my mind."

Carter had heard that statement, the declaration of ensuing madness rooted in some trauma or another, hundreds of times. Always some mundane obstacle in their lives. Something so trivial causing an uprooting of sanity. In Carter's earlier years, he pitied them. A dutiful desire to help those in need fueled his career. Some people he could help; others were simply coming to him as a means to admit their intent to themselves. They had already surrendered to lunacy. With the years though, came redundancy; with redundancy came apathy. Carter would hear tale after tale about a husband leaving, a wife cheating, a coworker being rude, a boss not giving the raise that was expected. His pity decayed into disgust at their weakness.

Everyone has problems, Carter would silently say to himself as he listened to his patients' fumbling accounts of their dilemmas. *How could these people,* he would think, *be so fragile as to collapse at the slightest inconvenience in their life.*

However, Carter's exterior dialogue was always the polar opposite to that of his inner judgments.

"It seems to me you're letting events out of your control take over your life."

Carter was beginning to have a routine. Where he used to listen carefully, approaching each patient as an individual with problems that are unique to them no matter how frivolous, he now had a speech that he recited to each patient. The same advice. The same tone. The same disinterest.

"You are living inside your own head. Most of these problems you manifest out of insecurity. Live in the now and own your actions.

Don't look to blame others for your emotional distress. It's time to take control."

Some patients would lie on that dreaded brown sofa and hear this spiel, genuinely attempting to apply the advice to their own predicaments. Some would entirely tune Carter out. They weren't here for advice, more just to vent and be heard. It didn't matter to Carter. It all paid the same, and it was all equally useless. These minds that Carter had deemed weak were no longer distressed souls in dire need of saving. Instead, they were all helpless idiots throwing their paychecks at him in hopes that he would justify their weakness with some sort of diagnosis.

This latest patient was no different. Another babbling weakling going on and on about losing their grip on reality. Explaining how everything around them was falling apart and how they had no clue how to stop it. Carter glanced over at the clock as nonchalantly as possible so as to not outwardly display his boredom.

"I don't hear my voice in my head anymore. My own thoughts are silent. It's more like images now. Images telling me what to do."

What was this? Carter quickly looked up from his notepad, which was entirely empty, barring a few doodles he'd made while pretending to make annotations.

"What do you mean you can't hear your voice? Can you elaborate?"

Carter was genuinely intrigued, which hadn't happened in years. Something different, a new ailment he had never heard described. This could at least make for interesting conversation while at work, something Carter craved immensely.

The patient's name was Trevor. He was relatively new, this only being his third visit to Carter. His first session was fairly basic. His thoughts were cluttered; he was unable to focus on important tasks. Things of that nature. His second was slightly less dull. He was beginning to have very negative thoughts, contemplating the repercussions of his suicide. Not out of the ordinary for Carter to hear on second sessions. But this. The third session was beginning to prove itself different.

"When I think." Trevor paused for a moment. Whether to find the right verbiage or to collect himself emotionally, Carter couldn't tell.

"When I think to myself, I don't hear my own voice anymore." The latter part of his statement was said through a squeaking voice attempting to fight back tears to no avail.

Carter looked more puzzled than sympathetic. "So your inner dialogue, it doesn't have a voice?" he asked plainly.

"It does. It's just not mine."

Carter looked on at the crying man, who was clearly distraught by the status of his psyche. Trevor's anguish wouldn't halt Carter's curiosity.

"And the images? You said something about images?"

Through his sniffles, Trevor began to respond, then briefly stopped to wipe his nose with his sleeve before starting up again.

"I see blurry images. I see them while I hear the voice. The voice is blurry too, but I can piece them together."

"What do the images usually entail?"

Trevor's submissive posture became even more abysmal as he cowered at the question. "I see bad things. And the voice, it says bad things."

How delightful! Carter exclaimed internally. Finally, someone actually crazy enough to keep him entertained during their session of complaints. Carter began to calm himself as he formed his next external statement.

"Are these things negative thoughts? Are they of physical harm?"

Carter hoped the inquiries would be like loaded questions to give him the best result. "Always violent. Always showing me, telling me." Trevor stopped.

Carter was on the edge of his seat with anticipation for the rest of Trevor's account. What else was the voice telling him? What else was it showing him? Carter had to know.

"What is it telling you, Trevor?"

Trevor buried his face into his palms as he sobbed out the rest of his horrors. "It's telling me to kill people."

The sobs were now uncontrollable. Carter was still enthralled, but nonetheless annoyed by the incessant crying.

"Calm down, Trevor. Just relax. You're in a safe place. Talk to me."

Trevor slowly raised his now-red tear-covered face from his hands, wiping at his nose again with his sleeve.

"I try to tell it no. I try to tell it to stop showing me these things, but when I think, nothing comes out. I can't speak to it to tell it to stop."

Pure, unhinged insanity. This was like a story Carter had seen on television or in a movie. Someone hearing terrible voices demanding that they kill others. Though Carter did wish to dig deeper into this psychosis, his legal obligation did have to take some precedence.

"Trevor, have you hurt anyone?"

Trevor's eyes shot up, meeting Carter's. This was the first time Trevor had taken his eyes off the floor all day. The crying stopped abruptly, and he sat silent, staring. The realization that Trevor was actually insane sank in for Carter. The concept that real danger was presenting itself at this moment. That concept became even clearer as Trevor began violently shaking while still sitting on Carter's old brown sofa.

"Trevor, are you okay?"

The shaking did not let up. Contrarily, it became worse as Trevor's breathing matched his body's sporadic motions. Quick breaths in and out of Trevor's nose were audible as he rattled on the sofa. Carter slowly rose from his chair, with a hand extended out as if to create a hopeless barrier between the two men.

"Trevor? Trevor, are you alright? Trevor?"

Carter's words were not premeditated at this point, he was more speaking purely on reaction to what he was witnessing. Then just as suddenly as it started, Trevor stopped. Gasping for air and looking around as if he'd forgotten where he was in the last few moments, Trevor's tears returned with a terrified look of confusion and pain.

"Wh—," Trevor started to say while retreating, his hands in front of his face to shield himself from something unknown. "What's going on? Where am I?"

Was this an elaborate game? Was Trevor pretending to be the victim of some sort of split personality disorder or some horrific supernatural force? Both of which Carter knew to be fake. Nonetheless, something was clearly very wrong here. The question simply being its legitimacy.

"Trevor, you are suffering from heavy psychological burdens right now. Your mind can't handle whatever it is you are going through. But I can help."

Carter attempted consoling the young man, less to make him feel comfortable and more to ensure that he didn't snap again. This time possibly leading to more violent ends.

"I want you to give me a call on my personal cell if you get symptoms this bad again. Can you do that for me, Trevor?"

Trevor's eyes didn't tell a story of lies or embellishment. They screamed out harrowing despair and revealed a man who had all but succumbed to a force beyond his understanding. Even more disturbing was that this was beyond Carter's understanding as well.

"I don't want to be alone anymore. I can't be alone with it."

The unease in Trevor's soft breaking voice was contagious. While still curious, Carter began to feel that something was truly wrong. Not a man desperately crying out for attention or a place to vent where he wouldn't be judged for not enduring his pain in a masculine silence. This was a man who had come to Carter for survival. A man in desperation.

"It? Trevor, you have to help me out here. You know there is no it. The thoughts you are having are coming from your subconscious. No one is telling you what to do."

Drenched in tears and sorrow, Trevor looked back at Carter, attempting to respond despite the lump in his throat.

"It …" Trevor paused, swallowing. "It is so loud."

"I know, Trevor. I know you're upset."

"No!" Trevor yelled back, trying to match the volume of the screeching in his head. "I'm not upset. I'm going to die."

"Trevor, you aren't going to di—"

Carter stopped. Blood. Blood running down Trevor's left cheek. A small, controlled stream spilling from the outer corner of Trevor's eye. Not like blood Carter had ever seen in his twenty-eight years. Darker, thicker. Trevor's left eye began to match the shade of dim red that coursed down his face. Carter's words were trapped behind a wall of dread; he was unable to piece together a coherent statement at the sight of the anomaly he was witnessing. As if the sanguine stream leaking from Trevor's eye had not distressed Carter enough, a voice Carter did not recognize escaped Trevor's mouth.

"Please, God, save me."

A distorted and inhuman call to a higher power that Carter did not believe in. Even so, Carter was not opposed to a god's intervention right now. Because this, whatever it was, was clearly out of the realm of his ability to help.

"Trevor, I'm going to call the hospital, okay? I think you're sick."

Carter's tone was an admission of his unease. He was shaken by the undeniable nature of what sat before him. Demons and monsters were never something Carter would have given any thought to. God wasn't real, much less a creature crawling in an eternal fire waiting to possess unsuspecting victims. But here it was. Right before him sat a man bleeding blackened blood from his dark eye and speaking in a vile voice that did not belong to him. All within a span of ten seconds, Carter went from worried that Trevor was clinically insane to horrified that Trevor may be under siege by something demonic in nature.

"Am I going to die?"

Trevor's right eye began to match the dull shade of his left. Carter pulled out his cell phone as casually as possible so as not to alarm Trevor.

"No, Trevor. You are going to be all right. We're gonna get you some help."

Carter raised the phone to his ear and explained the general situation to the dispatcher. Obviously, leaving out the bits that implied demonic possession so he would not be shrugged off as a prank caller. Carter simply stated the facts. Unnatural bleeding, discolored blood, and the address to come rescue this boy.

"They're on the way, Trevor. Sit tight."

Trevor was now squirming on the sofa, pain coursing through his veins along with the black blood.

"I won't! I won't!" Trevor cried out while writhing in agony.

"Trevor, what's going on? Trevor?" Carter shouted as he stood up, not sure if he should help or run away.

"I won't!" Trevor continued to cry while gripping his own face in a vain attempt to hold the pain at bay.

"Trevor!" Carter called out again, not knowing what else to do.

As Trevor rolled off the sofa to his knees, his head then whipped upward facing the ceiling as a monstrous voice roared out, "Kill him!"

The command given by the hidden malevolence within Trevor was followed by spewing gore. More of the grotesque inhuman blood erupted from Trevor's mouth coating the surrounding area. A hellish nightmare was unfolding in front of Carter. One he was helpless to stop.

"Leave him alone!" Carter screamed at the demon.

Without doubt or uncertainty, Carter knew that Trevor's soul was indeed being held hostage by an unearthly fiend. He could only watch as the beast ripped Trevor apart from the inside. Carter felt a helplessness that he never knew existed.

"God, please! Please, God, make it stop!" Trevor's shrieks of pain escaped his tortured body as he convulsed on the floor, still gurgling and dribbling plasma. Carter wondered what exactly God was waiting for. Now seemed as perfect a time as any to intervene.

"Trevor help is coming! Stay with me, Trevor, fight it!" Carter wasn't sure what he was saying anymore. Just whatever came to mind in these moments of distress. This was entirely uncharted territory. Perhaps a bible or a cross would help, but Carter was stuck regretting his decision to not keep those artifacts around the office.

Through Trevor's shouting and screeching, Carter could hear sirens approaching. Finally, he wouldn't be alone with this madness.

"They are almost here, Trevor. Hold on!"

Trevor's agony continued until the paramedics stormed the room to recover him. Even they were clearly distraught at the first sight of the blood-soaked scene in Carter's office. Perhaps the tame version of events Carter had told the dispatcher had not prepared the team of first responders for what was truly awaiting them.

Carter heaved a sigh of relief as he watched the team carry Trevor out, but he could still hear the screams until the ambulance raced away. The screams would stay in Carter's head for a few moments after that as well.

———

Days passed, and Carter didn't hear from Trevor. He was almost ashamed he never checked on Trevor's status at the hospital, but the fear of what answers might await kept him from doing so. The cleaning company that he hired to get rid of the copious amounts of bile and blood in his office reported the scene to the police. Despite Carter's explanation, the cleaners did not seem convinced. Reasonably so, Carter thought. The police arrived shortly after, and Carter explained in detail the horrific events that occurred. He didn't care anymore whether the police believed him or not. He knew what happened that day. He knew what he saw.

The police officer that Carter spoke to seemed surprisingly respectful when he heard the harrowing tale. He expected to be scoffed at, and perhaps even taken into custody for questioning, seeing as the room looked as though a murder had taken place in it. But instead of disbelief and judgment, Carter was shown what appeared to be genuine concern by the officer. Carter was pleased, up until the officers were leaving the scene, when he overheard the group of them calling him a nutcase. No matter, though. The police had been contacted. The room had been cleaned. Carter's run-in with this nightmare was over. He had done his part.

Three days had passed since the police visited Carter's office. Two days prior, Carter canceled all his appointments. He simply couldn't imagine sitting down across from that sofa yet again. Sitting down across from someone spilling their heart out, crying and begging for a solution to their plight. Someone in desperate need of support for their psyche. Not yet. He would need time to regroup his thoughts. He would need time to convince himself that the next client he saw whimpering on that sofa wouldn't begin to leak tears of blood and spew gore from their mouth while speaking in disembodied demonic voices. Nonetheless, bills needed to be paid, and clients needed to have their appointments kept, or they would find someone else to trauma-dump on. So on the third day after the incident, Carter was back in his chair, and back to faking concern for the mentally unstable sitters of his sofa.

It was a relatively busy day, seeing as a few clients from the previous two days had to be rescheduled, making for a jam-packed Friday. But he got through it the way he usually did: nodding his head and saying, "Hmm."

After six sessions of that routine, he was finished for the day. No demons, no monsters, no possessions or poltergeists. Just sad, broken people.

Carter made only one pit stop on his way home that night. He needed to pick up fast food. Unfortunately, he knew himself too well. No chance he would be cooking tonight. After eating half of his burger and finishing a second beer, he got in the shower. The shower was usually a place of reflection for him. He would lean his forehead against the wall while the warm water splashed against his back and neck. This was where he would ponder why he still did what he did. Why he bothered continuing with his profession. Not tonight, though. Tonight he wondered what happened to Trevor. Tonight Carter thought about the true well-being of someone else besides himself for the first time in recent memory. He decided that he would find out tomorrow.

***

Jolted awake, Carter's heart began to panic and race. He was thrown over onto his stomach, and he felt coarse, cold hands gripping his wrists tightly. What was going on? He knew this would have to come eventually. There was no way he could've seen the terrors that Trevor went through with that demonic entity, and it not then come for him as well. It was pulling his arms back behind him. Shouting in horror, begging to be left alone, Carter turned his head over to see what the creature that had subdued him looked like. His fear was then joined by shock and confusion at the sight of multiple men in what looked like biohazard suits. Covered head to toe by fabric and rubber, the men weren't demons, but still equally alarming to be assailed by in the middle of the night.

"What are you doing? Who are you?" Carter screamed as he tried to shake himself free from the yellow-suited men.

The men placed handcuffs firmly around Carter's wrists and concealed his head in a bag. Carter's shrieks of terror continued as he begged to be set free. Through his panic, he did notice the bag had holes for oxygen. Whoever these men were, they did not intend to kill him. Not yet anyway.

"Please! Please! I'll pay you anything, please! Please just let me go. I'll give you anything!"

Carter could have been convinced the kidnappers were deaf. They did not acknowledge his pleas for release and silently continued with their work. Now Carter was being lifted from his bed by two of the intruders. Either way, he would keep trying to call out. Even if these yellow men wouldn't respond, perhaps a neighbor would hear his cries for help. Unfortunately, the trespassers were aware of this possibility as well. Carter yelped out one last time to anyone who would listen before he fell unconscious. A strike to the temple with a baton instantly separated Carter's mind from reality and put him back to sleep.

Bright lights assaulted Carter's eyes as he slowly opened them. Meanwhile, he was feeling himself up and down to make sure all of him was still intact.

"Where am I?" Carter questioned to himself aloud.

He scanned the room for clues to his enclosure. Four white walls and a mirror. The room was about eight by eight feet. It seemed suspiciously like a jail cell. Even more concerning was the lack of a toilet, bed, or other features usually associated with confinement. So then, what was this?

"Hello? Where am I? Where have you taken me?" Carter continued calling out in relative confidence that behind the mirror stood an onlooker.

"Hello, Carter. I'm Special Agent Hudson. You're in a secure facility for monitoring the argus affliction."

The what? Carter was overloaded with information and had too many questions to be able to form a coherent thought. He began shooting glances around the room while his brain finally began to accept that he was being held captive.

"Let me out of here! Let me out. I haven't done anything!" Carter's heart began racing, on the brink of implosion as panic took hold of him.

"I'm afraid we can't do that, Carter. You're staying here with me." The voice was coming through an intercom but was still recognizably human. The intercom didn't distort or dull Agent Hudson's voice. Carter could hear every ounce of apathy coming from Hudson.

"Who the hell are you?" Carter yelled at the glass while standing up to confront his unseen captor.

"I told you that already, Carter. This is Special Agent Hudson."

"Special Agent? Like what, you're in the Secret Service?" Carter asked with notable sarcasm.

"FBI, Carter."

"FBI? What's the FBI want with me?" Carter was puzzled. The most recent event that would clearly seem related was obviously, Trevor. But the police had already come, interviewed, and inspected the scene. Perhaps they didn't believe Carter after all.

"I don't want you at all, Carter. I want to contain what's inside you."

"Inside me? What's inside me?" Carter was so baffled by the statement he forgot the obvious. The possession. Agent Hudson must be implying that Carter was now host to a demon, which had perhaps latched on to him when Trevor was at his office.

"Wait," Carter started while nervously pushing his fingers through his hair. "Does the FBI do exorcisms now?" He was half joking and half bewildered by the realization.

"No, Carter, we do not perform rituals here. I'm not here to banish a demon. I'm here to contain an outbreak."

The voice over the intercom only perplexed Carter even more. "Outbreak? Outbreak of what?"

"The argus," Agent Hudson replied plainly.

"Special Agent, I don't know what the argus is. I told the cops everything that happened. Trevor Wilcox was possessed by something. Something was speaking out of his mouth, something that was not him. And he started projectile-vomiting black blood all over my office! I don't know what the cops told you, but I didn't do anything!" Carter's angry monologue left him panting. Surely the FBI, of all people, was not holding him in this cell because he had seen a man possessed?

Carter waited for an answer for a few moments. Agent Hudson stood on the other side of the one-way mirror, sighing, preparing to dismantle everything Carter thought he knew.

"Well Carter, I've got some jarring news for you. Trevor was not possessed by a demon or devil or ghoul. He was infected with a parasite." Hudson paused for a moment to let Carter sit on the profound statement.

"A parasite?" Carter repeated.

"Yes. A parasite."

"A parasite made him spew blood and hear voices? The things he was telling me—he said he couldn't hear himself think anymore. What kind of parasite does that?" Carter was contemplating the idea when Hudson's response struck his ears like a dagger.

"None from this world."

"What? What do you mean?" Carter asked, still processing everything that was unfolding.

"It's straightforward, kid. It's not from Earth. The argus is alien."

The argus. That's what Hudson had said before. So that was the argus? An alien? None of this information answered more questions than it aroused.

"So Trevor had a parasite that was telling him to kill people? Why would it do that? How could it do that?"

Agent Hudson took a short break from answering Carter's incessant inquisitions to sip his coffee. After putting his beverage down, Hudson decided he would entertain Carter's curiosity a bit longer.

"We don't know exactly why. There's a few theories. It could be a parasite that attacks certain parts of the brain, and as a result, you lose cognitive function and perceive those violent thoughts. It could be the first wave before a full-scale invasion. A sort of preemptive strike to see how we react. Soften us up." Carter was listening in disbelief. This was an even more bizarre explanation for Trevor's symptoms than a possession. "I don't know exactly why or exactly how. All we know is once infected by the parasite, you can't hear yourself think. You start to hear a voice imposed by the parasite. Then you hemorrhage until you die. The parasite is so small you can't see it, and it multiples fast in the human body. We are fairly certain they are all hive minded as well. One of them will attempt to protect another one in locations where it should have no idea of its counterpart's predicament. That's why I believe it's here to conquer our planet. It seems too intelligent to simply be acting on primal instinct."

Carter heard everything, but stuck to one statement: Hemorrhage till you die. "So, Trevor? He died?"

"Yes, Carter. Not long after you last saw him."

"And I?"

"Yes, Carter. You will bleed to death in a few days."

Carter slammed his palms on the glass and screamed out to the agent who was merely inches away from him. "Get it out of me! Take it out!" he begged in terror at the thought of what happened to Trevor befalling himself.

"We can't. It's so small and reproduces so fast. You have thousands of them in you now. When the police put your statement on record, it hit all our flags, and we're lucky to have gotten to you when we did. You, the paramedics, your cleaning crew, and everyone at the hospital who came in contact with Trevor or his blood. All of you are walking bioweapons. It spreads fast and has a 100 percent lethality rate. The argus affliction has been spreading around for decades. Usually, we can get to the infected subject before they begin the more violent stages and spread it any farther. But sometimes not."

"So," Carter began in response to the death sentence he'd just been given, "I'm going to die a horrible painful death because of a parasite from space? I don't believe you. I simply can't. This is not real."

Even though the two men were speaking through an intercom, Carter could feel how little Hudson cared about his untimely demise. The Agent just listed over a dozen people who would have to suffer the same fate, and his voice didn't come with any comfort or remorse. He spoke about this impending doom as if it just was.

"I'm afraid it is real, Carter. It's not the only alien we've encountered either. Whether or not the others have any involvement with the spread of the argus affliction, we don't know. But I can tell you, it's all real. Whether you choose to believe it or not, it's going to take you in a matter of days."

Carter sat back against the wall he'd awoken on, the brightness of the lights still oppressing his eyes. It was still all too much. He still would not believe this wild tale of aliens and parasites.

"It was the devil that day. Trevor had the devil in him. I heard it tell him to kill me. I heard its voice. It was the devil." Carter's voice was defeated as he made this exclamation.

Agent Hudson looked down at Carter cowering on the floor and saw such a familiarity in him. He had seen it all before. The confusion. The resentment of the situation. And eventually, the denial of its reality entirely.

Hudson began to leave the observation room, but then he turned back to key up the intercom one last time.

"Everyone is so fearful of evil lurking beneath us. Following the dogma of old books made from superstition. So quick to suspect supernatural horrors and demons preying on them. It's uncanny to me honestly, that people would jump to such illogical and irrational conclusions before attempting any sort of explanation within the boundaries of what's possible. You don't have to look to ghosts and devils to find those unfathomable horrors. Instead look up, into the endless, and see that nothing at all, is everything all at once. The emptiness of the void that stares back at us is scary enough without your imaginary devils. Things worse than your devils live out there."

The Nightmare at Raek Manor

"With this revelation, things will be different next time."

The torn and stained fabric of the taxi made for an unpleasant ride. Two hours from the station seemed an unbearable journey home in this dilapidated cab. My feet were subjected to sudden bursts of freezing air that kept me from napping. From where this cold came from, I could not discover. My skin felt waves of cool chills that would have perhaps even been refreshing if it were not for my frigid feet. Maybe I was becoming ill? The sound of gulls squawking could be heard farther from the shore than I'd ever noticed before. I thought these were memories from behind my consciousness triggered by the sight of familiar trees and the smell of sea salt in the air. Yes, I was home.

I was summoned by my eldest brother, Franklin, to my father's estate some three days ago. Ramblings about emeralds and a fisherman. Nothing that seemed clearly rational or coherent. The piece of his diffuse pleas that finally caught my attention was the bit about our Father getting ill, or going insane. It seemed Franklin wasn't entirely sure which it was. Though I was never overly fond of Father—his heavy hand and judging eyes left a mark on my youth—I still loved him. A mean old man, to be sure, but my father nonetheless. So I loved him. Hearing the news of his diminishing health came as somewhat of a surprise, as the man had always been healthy. Active and strong for his age. In the middle of his Sixties, perhaps even the strongest of men will fold to time.

I was so entrenched in my thoughts I hadn't even noticed the cab rounding the driveway circle toward the front of my childhood house. A large out-of-date manor, belonging to a museum, if I had my way. The Romanesque architecture was one of excess, with large pillars towering between the stone stairs and the oak door of the entryway. Everything well kept, of course. But the cleanliness of the home's exterior could not hide the sorrows screaming from every window trying to get out. The place always had a way of looking grandiose while feeling harrowing. I tipped the cabman and stood before Raek Manor holding my suitcase. I was wearing a peacoat over my jacket, knowing the time of year would bring in the cold air from the sea, but I still felt those brisk chills against my skin. The frigid cold I had felt on my feet had not ceased either. I had predicted unease at the sight of this place, but this had surpassed my expectation. I heard Franklin calling out to me faintly. He must have seen my taxi arrive. I carried my luggage up the stairs toward the oak door that welcomed me into my past, opening the door without knocking. Perhaps rude, but I'd heard Franklin calling out, so my presence was known. Peculiarly, I searched the halls of the manor, calling back for Franklin to no avail. The large, high-ceiling rooms were full of art and trinkets, furniture meant more to be looked at than used. A place so full of things that still managed to be empty of any substance. As I came to the rear of the first floor, the windows were a portal dragging me backward in time to the most helpless age of my life. I had looked out those windows many times, staring at the sea, watching the waves break on the beach, the cold water menacing in its power and freedom. The waters taunted me as they came ashore and left at will. The idea of wading into them forever had crossed my mind more than once when I was a child.

"Oliver?" I heard Franklin's voice behind me, clear and concise this time.

I turned to see my brother, and his appearance nearly startled me. I could have guessed he had not been sleeping. The last time I'd seen Franklin, he sported a full head of hair and a sturdy frame. He was now holding as much weight but not near as impressively. His once-dark hair had begun to recede and hold patches of gray. Perhaps this was what the manor did to a person who never escaped it.

"It's good to see you, Franklin." His surprise at my standing in the rear foyer did confuse me, as he'd seen me arriving in the cab I was sure.

"When did you arrive?" Franklin's question immediately dismissed my previous thought.

"Not five minutes ago. I heard you calling to me. Did you not see my cab?"

Franklin looked lost. Perhaps from the events that had currently been unraveling, as well as by my insistence in hearing him call out to me.

"No, I saw no cab. Nor did I call to you."

"Well, perhaps it was just my mind playing tricks. Seeing this place has stirred up quite a few emotions already."

I began finding the hanger in the foyer for my peacoat. My thoughts betrayed me as I told myself I would refrain from seeing Cynthia if I had the ability. Now I had just barely begun to remove my coat when I found myself asking about her. Cynthia grew up with my brothers and me. She was the beautiful young daughter of our father's maid. The two of them had a room in the manor. Franklin, Johnathan, and I were all, of course, madly in love with Cynthia. The one source of joy that could be found in this wretched place. She had her pick of the lot, and she chose Johnathan. He was charismatic and the most handsome of us. Franklin and I were heartbroken, but we at least understood. Johnathan was the clear choice. A charming and humorous fellow, and the only one of us who never seemed to let the manor get to him. But for all the wonderful parts of my brother Johnathan, apparently, he was missing something inside. Some vitally important piece. Two years after I'd moved away from the manor, and four years after his marriage to Cynthia, he took his own life. I returned home for the funeral to mourn my brother, but I must selfishly admit my reasons were not that alone. With Johnathan gone, I knew Cynthia would now decide between Franklin and me. I must admit further still that when she chose Franklin, I was hurt far beyond when she chose Johnathan. Now it was not my most handsome brother being chosen by the girl I'd loved all my life, but I was the absolute last option when given the choice. Once it was clear to me that Franklin and Cynthia were to be together, I left the manor again. This time for good. Until nine years later. Until now.

"How is Cynthia? Is she home?" I asked as plainly as I could in an effort to seem nonchalant.

"Cynthia is dead." Franklin replied equally plainly.

"Dead?" My heart twisted in agony. No, surely she was not dead. "Dead how? Since when?"

"She committed suicide four years ago." Franklin could barely look at me; instead, his eyes scanned the floor. We both knew why.

Without Johnathan, Cynthia must have never felt truly whole. Franklin and I simply would not do. We could not make anyone happy. Us children of the manor. Us children of my father. Johnathan had a way of shutting out those terrible things. Not letting them alter his joyous demeanor. If not just on the outside, as it seemed through the years that he may have been harboring this pain internally. Franklin could not look at me when sharing this news because of his shame. A shame we both knew as a familiar partner. My sadness could only be measured in pain, as one can't truly measure something like grief or sorrow. The only way to have a rational understanding of one's sadness is to measure its pain against other tragedies in one's life. The agony my heart was wrenching in was far and past beyond all the torment that life had bestowed upon me up to now. The manor. My father. The sea that glared back and mocked me all those years. This was worse. To that end, I must realize now that those very perpetrators of my agony were the same vile nightmares that caused this. Without the manor, my father, and the dreaded sea, Johnathan may never have taken his own life; and in turn, Cynthia may still be alive.

"Franklin, my most sincere apologies. Why did you not tell me sooner?" For a moment, I had to put aside my sorrow for lost Cynthia and account for my brother's pain.

Franklin wrinkled his nose, as he usually does, a tick he's had since we were children. His eyes finally settled on one place, transfixed on the floor for a moment, before looking back up to me.

"I knew if I'd told you, you'd come back here, Oliver. I never wanted that for you. Never wanted to bring you back here."

I was perplexed by the sentiment, as it was quite contradictory to recent events.

"You'd call to have me come home for our father but not for Cynthia? Forgive me, brother, but that almost seems backwards."

Even now, while inside, the chill on my skin persisted. The freezing cold wrapping around my ankles now almost felt wet. I ignored it still.

Franklin dipped his head once more and sniffled, his nose undoubtedly making its trademark wrinkle. He looked back up to me with eyes that told me he did not have an answer for my inquiry. So I questioned no further on the subject.

After a few moments of silence, altered only by the ambient sea, I inquired about our father. "Where is the old man anyways? And I still am not quite sure I understand what you said was wrong with him."

"I'm still not sure either. Frankly, I wouldn't dare to guess." Franklin turned and began toward the stairs. I presumed he was taking me to father.

"You said he saw a fisherman? And emeralds? That was all I really gathered from our exchange."

"Yes, father saw the fisherman late one night, out by the water. Said the man was just standing there, wading in."

We continued up the stairs and then down the hall to the left, clearly headed toward the master bedroom. "What's a fisherman got to do with father's illness?"

"No clue," Franklin replied with frustration. "I never saw the man. Mr. Raek may just be going insane."

We reached the chamber of my ill father, and my spine tingled with resentment as Franklin's hand approached the doorknob. For the first time in almost ten years, I was about to see him. My indifferent father. Though upon entering, my emotions went from bitterness to what can only be described as dismay. My father lay on his bed, eyes so big I feared they might bulge out of his head. Spouting out whispers and breathing sporadically.

"Where are the maids? Why is he here unattended?" Though my hatred was beginning to show itself toward this man again, as before, I loved him still.

"I attend to him. All the maids have left."

I approached the bedside and looked down on what was once a proud, stoic man. Now reduced to whispers and panic.

"Left? Left why?" I demanded.

"Superstition, I suppose. One of them claimed to have seen the fisherman as well from the guest room window. They said he was standing out there one morning, out in the water."

"So? What superstition is that? A fisherman in the water? You wouldn't fear a farmer in his crop? They abandoned him because of this?" My anger was boiling over and seeping in with the puddles of confusion I was drowning in.

Franklin looked out of the window down at the breaking waves and let out a sigh of what I can only imagine was frustration that was equal to mine.

"It was after father saw the man and began his ramblings. He doesn't move now. Had we not brought him inside, he'd just be standing there still. Out in the water where he approached that man. When the maid saw him the next day, the fisherman, she went on about how he was a witch. About how father was trapped by him. Then they all left."

I wanted to rant about the disloyalty of the maids for a bit, but I was too busy attempting to put all the pieces together in my head.

"And what of the emeralds? You said something about emeralds?" Franklin looked back to me and then gestured a nod toward Father.

"Listen to him."

I sat on the bed next to my mumbling father and slowly lowered an ear to meet his whispers. At first it was nothing. Just gibberish, I suppose. But the words slowly began to find themselves, and I wish they hadn't.

"Behind the isles the emeralds offer hollow, inside the isles the emeralds taste a soul and swallow."

I listened closely to his rhetoric a few more times, only to hear he was repeating this phrase. Though it was undoubtedly nonsense, something about it I found intrinsically disturbing. More off-putting still, I could swear I'd heard this before. There was a familiarity in its strange manner. The cold whooshing through my feet had come back to me, and the whisk of cool air upon my entire body joined it.

"Franklin, I would be lying to you if I did not say I think something not entirely normal is going on here."

Franklin wrinkled his nose before responding.

"Yes Oliver, I agree. That's why I called you. Otherwise, I would have never brought you back here. I know how much you hate this place. And I wouldn't damn you one minute longer here than is absolutely necessary."

I felt guilt crawling up my chest and through my throat, as if it wanted to confess itself to my brother right then. But I calmly stopped it. He was, of course, my older brother, so I should not be shocked by his concern for my well-being. However, I could not help but feel wrong for missing my dear Cynthia. His dear Cynthia. I could not help feeling guilty for she was the true meaning of my return. Regardless now, she was buried, my father was comatose, and my brother needed my assistance. As penance for my deception, I would stay and see this through.

"Thank you, brother. I again express my sorrows for your dear wife, as well as for your current predicament. Being left here alone with Father like this is a shameful act. All the maids who left shall never be reinstated here or receive another dime from our father."

I stood up from the bedside as I continued my pronouncement. "You are right, I do fundamentally despise this place. All our good memories here are dead now. I would like to leave as soon as possible, but I assure you I will not leave before Father's condition improves. You will not be alone in this."

That night I stayed in a guest room. My childhood bedroom would only have fostered nightmares. My sleep was restless all the same, however. The cool gusts against my skin, my feet going frigid through the night. Even more strange was I could swear I was hearing things. The gulls sounded so vivid, as if they were right there. I could hear Franklin's voice calling out to me. The worst of these hallucinations was the sound of the dreaded sea, breaking its waves. I could hear it all night, as if I were afloat at that very moment. It was just then that I decided that this would be the last time. I shall never return to this place. I shall find this fisherman and leave Raek Manor for good. I shall never return to this place.

The morning brought with it relief, as the nights in the manor were always grim. I got out of bed and faced the window, to face my nemesis. But where I thought I'd look upon a lifeless sea staring menacingly back at me, I instead caught glimpse of a man standing at the sea's edge. Just standing in the waters as the waves broke just below his knees. His coat and his hat were undoubtedly that of a fisherman. I quickly dressed myself in yesterday's clothes, not wasting any time to grab new garments out of my suitcase. Wanting to catch this man before he disappeared to ask him what business he had here, I ran for the bedroom door. I thundered down the staircase, surely loud enough to have awoken Franklin, but I did not have time to wait. I bolted out the back door toward the sea, too fast to retrieve my peacoat.

To my delight, the man was still in the water. Part of me was worried he would be gone by the time I'd made it downstairs and out the back of the house. It was at this moment, however, that my haste turned to restraint. I was still walking toward the man wading in the water, just without the same vigor. Thoughts crept into my mind like a shadow through a window at sunset. Why was this man out here alone?

Where had he been staying? The Raek estate goes on for a hundred acres in both directions from the beach. What the maid had claimed about this fisherman, to be a witch or some sort. When had he arrived? Late at night? Just standing in the water? For what reason? I no longer wished to question this man. Instead, I moved forward to get this over with, so I could return home. My real home. Not this place. The tantalizing sea was still staring back at me. A cool dew that glanced over top of the water greeted me on my approach. Without my peacoat, I could feel the mist right through my clothes, and it was gently refreshing on my skin. The gulls antagonized from above, and as I stepped into the cold water, the chill was not at all unfamiliar.

"Sir, hello?" I called out to the fisherman. "What is it you're doing out here?"

He did not respond to me. I took a few more waded steps. Something in my gut told me to run. Something in my being told me to flee from this place. From this man. I still could not see his face but his posture alarmed me. His arms and hands had no natural hang to them. He was almost stiff. I dared not make any assumptions on why the water grew colder still the nearer I got to the man. In the distance, I could hear Franklin calling out. Perhaps wondering where I'd gone. I wanted to go to him then, to turn away from this strange man and run to Franklin. I elected not to. I would make due on my promise to my brother.

"Sir, you spoke to my father, and he fell quite ill afterward. Can you please tell me what you two discussed?"

The fisherman's lack of a response found its way to me as rude and distressing. "Sir! Can you hear me? Sir!"

The waters were now bordering on freezing, my feet completely numbed by it. The dew was still glistening on my face. Then I thought of this moment. Something began to overcome me. I'd heard those words before, whispered to me by my father. I'd heard them before because I'd spoken them.

My pondering was interrupted as the man's head began to turn toward me. The sounds presented by the twisting of his neck were crunching and snapping, as though he was breaking a rigid object. Until his eyes were revealed to me, I had not yet become fully irrational. It was when the fisherman glared into me, showing that he was no fisherman at all, that I lost my grip on reality. In his face were features I wished I would soon forget but knew better. There was nothing human about this thing, except the placement of the eyes. The eyes sat there as if to deceive you from afar, but at a closer glance, I could see it was anything but a man. What would perhaps pass as skin for this being was a tight layer of pale-gray leather, which carried with it no softness, as you would expect on a face with normal flesh. The eyes shone with an emerald glow—both piercing and alluring. Though every ounce of sanity that had not been drained from me yet screamed for me to look away, I could not. Then without my own consent, my mouth opened and uttered the phrase.

"Behind the isles the emeralds offer hollow, inside the isles the emeralds taste a soul and swallow."

My muscles felt a tenseness I could not have predicted, even from memories of my most horrific nightmares. Even if I'd willed it with every last ounce of my soul, I could not choose to run away now. Just as looking into its emerald eyes gave the monster dominion over my voice; my body was now its jurisdiction too. It was as though I were looking upon a crashing meteor plummeting through the clouds, something inevitably dooming. But this doomed fate was mine alone. No one to share this dreaded moment with. My very own inevitable catastrophe unfolding before me, with the kind of world-ending horror that could only be felt when its very existence was revealed before your eyes but refuses to strike until you've had ample time to digest exactly how dire the situation is. Somehow the gravity of its gaze found its way not just to my eyes but my ears as well, as in a strange impossible way I could hear its call. It sounded like the faint ringing you sometimes get in your ears, while the distinct gleam of its eyes had its own different sound entirely. In hearing this sound, and seeing the glimmering of its emerald eyes, I had a sensory triggered memory. This was not the first time I'd waded into ominous cold waters that grinned malevolently as they knew the beast they harbored. This was not the first time the fisherman turned to confess his more sinister existence to me, and stared through my eyes into my soul with those ghastly emeralds. This was my fate, and it was not the first time I'd experienced it. This creature had me, just as it had my father. It had me here in the water with him, to do what I must assume would be a malicious task. The thought that what lay before my eyes now may be a mere remnant of my memories found its way to me as more frightening than the very sight I was seeing itself, as the very nature of this thought implied something worse may truly be happening to my flesh and bones in this moment. Something I was not meant to struggle against so this demon of emeralds and corrupt waters may practice its ritual unopposed.

If I could have perhaps heeded the warning in the back of my subconscious, and not ignored the signs, I may have avoided the paralyzing gaze of the fiend. My body and consciousness could be freed of the witch's authority if I was able to look away from the emeralds glow.

With my last bit of conscious will, I mustered the strength to regain dominion over my voice and pronounced to the emerald eyed witch, "With this revelation, things will be different next time."

BEGUILE

The world I'd awoken to was different from where I'd left off. My exploration of a habitable asteroid was abruptly ended by my anatomy's untimely decay.

As my consciousness slipped into ephemeral dormancy, my flesh constituted its replacement. My familiarity with existence's different presentation from a smaller perspective prepared me for a certain change in outlook. But this—this was entirely a different setting. No longer on the asteroid. Based on the atmosphere, I knew I was more than likely on a fully rotational planet or moon. Furthermore, based on the atypical structure I was confined to, I knew I had more than likely been found and taken during my short hibernation by sentient life.

Perhaps I was found and "rescued" by a life-form. A life-form that apparently came to the bold conclusion that I was deceased based on my motionless flesh. But why, then, would I be restrained? A small cubic room with clear glass three-quarters of the way up the wall on one side and artificial lights overhead. I was strapped to a small platform in the middle of this room. The barbarism of this predicament had me slightly worried. What sort of savage sentient would find, then confine, another existence like this?

No sooner had I formed my inquiry than I had my conclusion. Through the window and into my sight glided three life-forms. I was unable to see the lower half of their bodies, but from what the upper half told me, they were poorly evolved creatures. Full of joints and easily breakable appendages—a design that showed limited movement. A soft but tight outer layer seemed spread across their entire body, barring a few apertures. I could only hope a hard framework was not beneath that layer, as that would make for such an easily lacerated outer shell. And certainly, the two exposed organs sitting atop the body were not their visual mechanism? After observing them for a brief moment, my conclusion was that the exposed organs were indeed the creatures' means of sight.

Despite my current primitive confinement, I had to assume these creatures were vastly intelligent to have survived and evolved among the other life-forms of their origin planet without being exterminated with such poor and feeble design. Or, of course, the rest of the life on their origin world could have been extremely crude.

One of the three was clearly in charge. Tribalism is a telltale sign of barbaric life. I would just have to hope that all the unpleasant signs I'd witnessed in this short period were merely coincidental. I was easily able to pick up the sound waves their communication was emitting. After a few exchanges of dialect, I was able to decipher most of the creature's communicative language. So it appeared the director of these life-forms had commanded one of the others to study me?

To say I was confused would be an understatement. Maybe even I misinterpreted my own comprehension of how I perceived this. Perhaps I was not confused but, more likely, excessively disappointed. Another sentient world-traveling life-form, capable of traversing the endless black, was mindless enough to study me, or any existence it found, for that matter. I quickly concluded this species' origin world was populated with only simple life. Perhaps even only organisms that operated off a primordial food chain, simply living to ingest and not be ingested. I had visited worlds like that before. Even so, none of those worlds had life that was intelligent, or intelligent enough to travel out of their crevice in the void and venture outward anyways.

Another alarming sight was the awe-stricken subordinate of the director. The one who had been bestowed the task of investigating my existence. He was clearly meant to be an intellectual superior to his two companions. That was why he was chosen for this task. But if this was the peak of their intellect, I may be doomed. As I continued to decode their dialect, I was finally able to put all the pieces together regarding the discussion before me.

"Well, General, this is by far the biggest scientific, biological discovery of not just our lifetime but of all time. I thank you for the opportunity."

"Don't mention it, Pyke. You just do your job and tell us everything we need to know about this thing," the director, who I now knew as General, responded to the ignorant intellectual. "Just remember, like I told you son. You've got four weeks to give us something to chew on. Just enough information to keep the suits back at home happy, and this thing's all yours to poke and prod. Can you do that?"

Poke and prod? What kind of savagery was this? They couldn't seriously intend to learn anything about me through such primal means. How could it not occur to them to simply attempt communication? My thoughts were interrupted by the continued dialogue.

"Yes, sir, I can do that for you. First things first, I'll need a sample of its tissue, but there's no telling how dangerous it is. I don't want you sending anyone in there until it's unconscious again. I know it's a lot smaller than its momma, but it's not worth the risk until we know what it's capable of."

What sort of moronic delusion was this primitive creature babbling? This was the smartest among them? This fiend would take a piece of my flesh before even attempting communication with me? Furthermore, it made the bold assumption that the carcass they found me in was my progenitor in ancestry. How could someone with an affiliation of intelligence make such a wild and outlandish claim with zero context?

Through my baffled ramblings to myself, I failed to notice the textural change in the atmosphere. The creatures. The captors. They released something into the room. Something to make my consciousness fade. I knew this because the moron himself told me his plan under the arrogant conclusion that there must be no way I could possibly understand their dialect. But now I noticed. The three confused individuals stared in at me, watching the gaseous substance fill the room. I quickly feigned a loss of consciousness. Surely, beings dull enough to assume this substance would cause me loss of function were also naive enough to assume my dormancy meant they had achieved their goal.

To absolutely no bewilderment from me, my captors acted accordingly. I was unsure of their plan beyond that of taking some of my "tissue," but I could only hope they would not kill me in the process. Any being not comprehensive enough to understand my life cycle of forming new cells to create another body to pass my consciousness into, leaving behind my old dying cells, couldn't be trusted not to assume a sample of my flesh was not a vital part of my anatomy, severing it from my soon-to-be cadaver. Hopefully, the beast would just cut out a piece of redundant tissue. Painful, to be sure. But unavoidable, to be just as sure.

Three unknown members of their species had entered my containment in suits that covered their flesh entirely, as though they feared being in the same room as me could cause harm. This led me to conclude that the creatures were easily susceptible to infestation from viruses and parasites, in which case I was surprised they would be smart enough to take that precaution. The three that stood outside the glass stared in at me with amazement as the three inside attempted to steal a piece of me in the name of science. One of the suited beings inside my confinement came close and stood over me, wielding a small apparatus. Then I was struck simultaneously by disbelief and offense when the primitive beast pressed the apparatus to my outer layer and dragged the tip in a ridiculous attempt to puncture me.

This was how they intended to get a sample of my tissue? Some crudely made device to literally pierce my body and mangle a piece of me out? Additionally, these beings even thinking my form was feeble enough to puncture with such primitive tools offended me. But my offense was their excitement.

"Is it some kind of shell?" the General asked his subordinates.

Before any of them could answer him, Pyke spoke up to clarify his hypothesis of me.

"It's an exoskeleton. It's hardened on the outside to protect it from damage. Makes sense for something you'd find out in such harsh conditions."

I wanted to be impressed, but the conclusion basically presented itself to Pyke. An obvious observation. Nonetheless, these science-seeking zealots would not give up so easily in their barbarous quest for a piece of me to examine. The three butchers inside left and then promptly returned with a new tool. This one was seeming slightly more evolved. A grip made to be easily wielded by their multipronged extremities. The bolder of the three approached again, now using this new tool that seemingly stimulated molecules to produce a beam of light that emitted focused radiation. The beam cleanly burned through my flesh, and I was soon missing a small circular portion of my existence. Now it belonged to them. This would mark the beginning. This was the moment I knew conclusively that these creatures meant me physical harm and would kill me if left to their own devices.

The one in charge of researching me was called Pyke. He was a scientist in their culture. Pyke was clearly baffled by my form, and more confusing still, he seemed to assume many things about me based purely on his perspective of my image.

My lack of exposed organs atop my body led him to believe I had no visual photoreceptors. I do. My lack of vocalization made him believe I can't communicate. I can. My continued life without any substance that was visible to Pyke led him to one conclusion, which I did admire, though. Pyke was able to deduce that I survived on cellular division, and that small trace amounts of basic elements I took in through my skin fueled this system. My growth into a matured form was not much unlike his own, making this deduction not too hard to comprehend for narrow-minded Pyke, but still, I was almost proud that the poor would-be intellectual could figure out how I fueled my body, seeing as it was a foreign concept to his own survival.

The first few days that passed, I had no choice but to bide my time. I was still too small to engage in any investigation of my predicament, as I was still confined by my restraints. During this time, though, Pyke reveled in his research into my life. He would spend countless hours examining my extracted flesh on his side of the glass, making all sorts of notes and notions about what he had discovered in my cells.

Apparently, I also grew at a "rapid pace" in the eyes of this intellectual. The concept of perspective seemed so aloof to these beings it was almost uncanny. I had grown large enough to nearly encompass the entire platform they had restrained me to when they first brought me here. Unbeknownst to Pyke, his commentary on my form's expansion gave me a pertinent piece of information to my escape.

"In just one week's time, the life-form has over sextupled in size. It's already near what I can only assume is adulthood based on the body of the dead mother."

Pyke dictated his findings into a device that I believed recorded his speech for later listening. But the important piece of knowledge he had delivered to me was my timeline. I now knew the length of time to complete a full "week" based on how long it had been since I first woke up here, to now. The General had told Pyke he had four weeks. Four weeks to discover my anatomy's information. I could only assume that at the end of this time frame, I would either be disposed of or subjected to some other undesired fate. I deduced "four" quickly. It was a numerical concept, and deducing how many four was did not take long as Pyke noted I had four appendages just as his species did. But a week. This time concept eluded me until now. With my newfound knowledge of my timeline, I could act accordingly. Suddenly, though, through Pyke's rambling dialogue, he caught my attention.

"After further examination of the adult corpse, though, I can no longer say with confidence that it is this creature's mother, or parent of any kind."

What was this? Was dear Pyke smarter than I'd given him credit for? He continued relaying his thoughts into his device while pacing around, as if the excitement of his discoveries gave nervous energy that could only be released through movement.

"It's nothing like anything I've ever seen before. But it appears less like a birth, and more like a growth. There was no embryo. The corpse has no signs of organs for procreation. I don't think the new life form is a baby at all, but more an extension of the previous creature."

Well, well, Pyke was not as dull as I previously perceived. Perhaps these creature's presumptive nature had influenced me into making the same mistake. I would not make that error again. The last thing I could do was underestimate them.

Pyke walked closely to the glass that divided us, staring in curiously, but now more cautiously than he had before, as he made one final memorandum in his current recording.

"Ever since I discovered the creature's method of sustaining itself, I've been trying to figure out what about gas would cause loss of consciousness. We gassed the room in order to retrieve a tissue sample, and the creature was affected quickly; but so far, I've concluded that based on its anatomy, there is no explainable reason the gas should have caused unconsciousness."

Pyke stared in at me, and I, without his knowledge, back at him.

"It is possible there is something I have not discovered yet regarding the effect of gas on the subject, but another possibility I can't ignore has presented itself. The subject may have been faking the effect."

We were now both aware. While Pyke was still not entirely sure, his suspicion alone changed the dynamic of my situation. If he figured out my level of intelligence, who knew what he would do. Or more so, what the General will do once the information is relayed to him. The game was now truly in motion.

My plan up to that point, was to show signs of rudimentary intelligence. The more intrigued Pyke became, the more tests he would want to run. With more tests would come more opportunities for me to learn something about him, or about my confinement. The real goal at hand was escaping this prison of "science," But things had gotten more complicated with Pyke's recent suspicions. The plan remained relatively the same, but I could not give away my true cognitive ability. I would have to be selective in the levels of intelligence I showed.

The goal in its most basic form was to escape this room first. Over Pyke's most recent break from analyzing me, as he retires often for long intervals before returning, showing signs of grogginess implying that this species slept regularly, I grew large enough to tear clean through the restraints that held my motion at bay. I knew there must be devices watching me at all times, so I searched the room for obvious escapes, while appearing to just wander aimlessly so as to not create suspicion.

Once I was out of this box, once I was free, escaping would be fairly simple. I had little to no doubt they would vastly underestimate our physical strength disparity. I had watched Pyke struggle to move small equipment, and I had also gathered the beings known as "humans" operate their body on a system of leveraging tissues that act independently of one another while attached at the joints. I could see it in their form—when they moved, when they conducted tasks, each piece of tissue operating beneath their soft layer stretched over their hard frame. This was a system I could easily exploit. Snapping those extremities would prove easy, and the tolerance of bodily impairment seemed to be extremely low in these humans. Two visits ago from Pyke, I witnessed him collide his knee into the platform used to maintain his devices. Pyke cried out in pain and gripped at the knee, for what seemed to be a concerning amount of time for such a small dilemma. This species, humans, were indeed feeble. It would not be an issue of physical means; instead, I would simply need to outwit them.

The General had visited Pyke a few times in the first week of my captivity, usually accompanied by the third being that I'd awoken to that day who stood alongside them, who I now knew was some sort of guard to the General. Yes, a guard. I wanted to believe at first this was because we were positioned somewhere that a hostile organism may attack at any given moment, but I soon learned through my listening that these beings practiced interspecies war. How surprising.

This most recent visit from the General, however, proved to be enlightening. The interest in me had only grown now that the humans had seen the rate of my growth compared to their own. As well, they were intrigued by my body's method of movement, as it was alien to them. One connected flesh, flexible and capable of contortions unnatural to them. No flawed designs causing hyperextension when I twisted my extremities. On top of my physical attributes, the General was interested in some of the information that Pyke relayed to him.

"Its body is almost like one massive muscle. Its limbs can rotate with near impunity. The only thing that really seems to limit its ability to contort is the exoskeleton, but even that is insanely flexible for how durable it is."

The General looked in at me, his stares joined by his companion and Pyke as well. Though, the General was harder to read. His intentions were not yet entirely clear. Certainly, he wished to know more about me, but to what end? Pyke seemed driven by a sense of wonder. A desire to simply learn. The General, however, seemed to have an agenda. Like this was not at all for the sake of knowledge itself. His sternness implied he had a very specific goal. Just not a goal I could deduce at that very moment.

"You said one muscle, Pyke?" the General said with his eyes still examining me.

"Yes. That's right."

"How strong would you say it is? Is it dangerous?"

My size alone compared to the humans implied I would be extremely dangerous to them, seeing as I was roughly double their weight. But the General wanted specifics, it seemed.

"It is highly dangerous," Pyke answered plainly. "If it got a hold of you, it could, more than likely, rip you in half. Fairly easily at that."

The General stood staring, not fazed by the statement. His companion, however, turned his attention toward Pyke, seemingly alarmed by the idea of me pulling him apart.

"Skin tough as stone and strong enough to tear a man to pieces. That's a tough customer."

His line of questioning and general interest in my physical capabilities began to make me suspect his motives. Without certainty, I theorized that he wished to use me for violent means. Time would tell.

"Certainly, sir," Pyke replied.

Curiously, Pyke did not mention to the General his concern about the possibility of my sentience. I figured that would be at the forefront of the conversation today. Perhaps Pyke had an ulterior motive of his own.

Another monotonous period passed, where Pyke left me to my pondering as he departed for his required rest. Though boring, it proved a perfect time to contemplate my escape options. I'm nearly ashamed to admit the idea flickered in my head for a brief moment that maybe I should just ask Pyke to let me go. From one knowledge seeker to another. My own kind would be disgusted with my foolishness if they knew I'd even considered revealing myself to the humans. Revealing what kind of intelligence I possessed to these monsters now would mean more than suicide. Without a doubt, I would be subjected to horrific bodily harm and brought to the brink of my pain threshold daily until my body could take no more. No, simply asking would not do. But I did have a plan.

My train of thought was abruptly ended by Pyke's office door swinging open. Through my window, I could see Pyke and the General walk in to the room, flipping the lights on and scribbling down notes. Pyke often made his notes on a script to give them to the General at a later time. But what was all this? The two men were here well past the usual study hours, not to mention seeing the General twice in one day was highly irregular.

"All right, Pyke, I have Ramirez suited up and ready for subject retrieval. You tell me when and I'll send him in."

Did the General just say subject retrieval? They were going to send someone in here? This would be much easier than I thought.

"Yes, sir, I'm going to give it enough gas to drop an elephant. Don't wanna risk anything. When the subject appears sedated, I'll give the mark."

Poor Pyke. I'd heard him time and time again go on about how this discovery would change the course of human history. Based on how the few humans I'd seen were nearly entirely reliant on their social structure, I deduced that as a whole, their species was one of competition and titles. A race of animals who were in a continuous contest to prove their own worth. Surely, this was going to be Pyke's crowning achievement. The one that would win him his title. Perhaps one day, though, these humans would understand. True intelligence did not come from a competitive drive but from a humble curiosity. The ability to understand that you may not understand is the true first step to allowing your mind to take in all information as it comes—instead of insisting on infecting information with your biases as these humans do. However, whether that day ever came was of no concern to me. This would be the last time I would interact with this species. For the next few thousand years minimum anyways. Perhaps by then, I would have forgiven these atrocities.

"Ramirez, stand by," the General ordered via radio.

"Standing by, sir," I could hear the General's guard respond, who I now knew by the name of Ramirez.

"Gas is going in, give it a minute. I'll give you the signal." Pyke had a stern confidence backing his words.

Just as before when this gaseous substance entered my quarantine, I could feel the change in my skin as I absorbed it. Of course, it didn't harm me in the slightest. But I will play along. Just like last time. I will play along. The major difference this time is my size. The human's error will prove deadly for the ones entering. The concept of forcibly ending sentient life appalls me. It's perhaps the rarest thing in the entire universe. The circumstance just requires it. If I want to escape this place, I will have to match the humans in their barbarism.

I began to show slight signs of fatigue. Stumbling, leaning against the walls of my containment for support. Then I gave out. Whisked away in a deep coma. One that I was ready to snap out of the moment I saw the door to my enclosure open. I would grab Ramirez, crush him, then find my way through the human compound until I could get outside into the elements. From there my options would be to steal a human craft or use raw materials I find to create a device so I may communicate my predicament with my kind.

"All right, Ramirez, you're up."

Pyke's words would be a death sentence for this poor creature, who was ignorantly entering a containment with a life-form he didn't understand. The sound of locking mechanisms unbolting was followed by the sudden sliding open of my gateway to freedom.

As I previously predicted the humans would miscalculate my strength, they also must have miscalculated my speed. My four extremities worked seamlessly together, rotating quickly to propel my pseudo-dormant body toward the door before I could even see Ramirez. As I passed through the doorway, I could see a wall straight ahead of me. The passageway would lead to either side of me horizontally. I quickly leaped to one side, but to my confusion, there was another wall. A strange architectural choice? My anatomy's structure allowed for agile and quick directional changes, but as I jolted in the reverse direction, that corridor too was sealed off by yet another unsuspected wall. Confusion set in for a mere moment. Until my realization took hold. Pyke.

"My God, Pyke," I could hear the General commend him.

So this was Pyke's plan. He wouldn't ask me whether I was sentient, but deceive me into admitting it.

"I …" Pyke began to stammer. "I can't believe it. I had my suspicions, but I can't believe it."

The General grabbed a hold of Pyke's feeling appendages using his own while congratulating him. "I thought you were going crazy on us, Pyke, truly. But this is astounding work. Great job."

"Do you know what this means?" Pyke fired back quickly, now gripping at his own flesh atop his form. "The least likely answer is it has encountered humans before. The much higher probability is that it's been listening this whole time and was able to decode our dialect in a matter of days. Perhaps even hours."

Mere moments, Pyke. I did it in mere moments. However, semantics aside, my underestimation of Pyke has now revealed me. Pyke suspected I had faked my unconscious state when he had first filled my enclosure with that gaseous substance. By presenting this scenario to me and gassing the room once more, Pyke merely wanted to observe, to see how I would react, and I took the bait. I have been outsmarted by a primal brute.

"That's extremely impressive, Pyke. Do you think that means it can talk to us?" the General inquired.

"I have no idea. But, sir, I can tell you that this thing is far more dangerous than we anticipated or could have prepared for. The unknowns here are far too great. We have to kill it."

And so we had to come to this. The humans had discovered that my intelligence could perhaps rival their own and decided that in itself was too great a threat. All acts of vile barbarism and savagery up to this point could not compare to what I'd just heard. A species that couldn't stand on even terms with anything, a species that must look down upon all other life. Anything viewed as an intellectual equivalent is a threat to be snuffed out.

"Kill it? Pyke, be rational. This thing is worth billions. We'd both be put on trial for destruction of government property. It would be the end of us. It's out of the question."

I quickly reconsidered my previous statement about Pyke's most recent comment being unrivaled in its uncivilized nature. The General took that title with haste.

"Sir, I don't think you understand." Pyke stared in at me, no longer amused by what he saw. Now he looked at me with the dismay of a being who understands its place at the apex is under contention. "If it can decode our language by merely listening, there's absolutely no telling the limits of its intelligence. I'm telling you, if you leave this thing in here, it is going to get out. People will die."

Although my perspective on the situation was a polar opposite to Pyke's, I could not in good conscience deny his claim. If I was left in here trapped like an animal, I would escape, and I would end the life cycle of any humans attempting to stop me. However, my deductions had been nearly spot on to this point, barring my second underestimation of Pyke. The General would not allow me to be killed. I was valuable in the culture of these pride gluttons.

"It's out of the question, Pyke. Clearly, you've got its number. You've been watching it, you know more about it than any of us. So it's up to you to ensure it doesn't escape. Got it?" The General was firm in his declaration. I was not to be destroyed.

Clearly, Pyke had voiced his suspicions to the General in private, wisely, to prevent me from just playing dumb when the time came to test his theory. Walls were quietly set up just outside my enclosure, which I was foolish enough to miss. I had become so transfixed on studying Pyke that I let something so blatantly obvious slip my detection. Had I been more vigilant, I would have deduced that the irregular sounds outside my walls required further contemplation before I should attempt such a rash escape. It seems the ignorance of humans is truly contagious. Perhaps the humans themselves began as a parasite in their world.

"Sir, please, you don't under—"

"That's final, Pyke. The subject will be kept alive. Do you understand?" The General's interruption showed his agitation with Pyke's repeated request to annihilate me.

"Yes. Yes, sir, I understand."

Pyke and I looked to each other. We looked at each other with undeniable certainty that only one of us would survive this.

The next few days were far different than our previous interactions. Firstly due to Pyke having to examine me through glass across a room through a passageway, when I so chose to reveal myself to him. I knew better than to reenter the previous room. Though much smaller, my space in the corridor would have to be my new habitat. Moving back to my previous cage would surely lead to the gateway closing behind me, allowing for a multi-sealed entrance to my enclosure. I needed as few doors barring my escape as possible. That being noted, I still did have to make myself visible through the doorway fairly often. Though I could hear Pyke, I could not see him unless I allowed him to see me.

Pyke's examinations were no longer filled with awe and inspiration, but, instead, with a fearful carefulness. Attempting to discover any detail that may lead him closer to understanding how to control me I presume. Or perhaps gain an upper hand if I were to escape.

Half a week after the detection of my intellect by the humans, the General returned. It had been the longest stretch of consecutive time without a visit from him.

"Well, Pyke, the board is ecstatic. You've wowed them."

"Thank you, General." Pyke replied reluctantly.

"We have received a report that you are to attempt communication today."

What was this? Had the General somehow made a discovery of his own? Or was this a blind attempt at a broad speculation?

"Sir?" Pyke seemed baffled by the mere acknowledgment of the possibility that I could recite the human dialect back to them. "We have absolutely no reason to believe it can talk. Even dogs can understand some basic words. That doesn't mean it's going to start calling out to you when it wants to go for a walk."

No information on dogs. I would need further information to comment on Pyke's previous implication.

"You said it yourself. No telling how smart it really can be. No harm done in trying, right?" The General was optimistic. Perhaps my ability to communicate would be groundbreaking for them. How pitiful.

Pyke looked toward me, then back at the General, with some hesitation, then once more back to me.

"I suppose not." Pyke sighed.

I stood in the doorframe, looking back at Pyke. I wanted to see his expressions while he spoke. The human face is full of muscles that seem to almost involuntarily emote when a person is speaking, revealing the true feelings behind their communication. Clearly another terrible design flaw, but had this species been less barbaric, there would be something almost endearing about this property.

"Can you," Pyke began, before pausing and wincing slightly. "I know you can understand me. If you can respond, do so now. We can discuss your potential release."

Wow, how enticing. Surely this wasn't an empty gesture to coerce me into vocalizing.

"I don't want to keep you here anymore. If you can speak to me, do it now. This is your chance."

My chance. Of course. Because the implication was if I didn't speak, I would remain a captive forever.

"If you don't speak up now, your entire race will be—"

"Enough Pyke!" The General pushed at Pyke's torso while he shouted.

My entire race? What about my race? Surely there was no way the humans had found my origin world.

"You keep your mouth shut. And if I hear anything like this again, if you disclose anything, you will be executed for releasing clearance 5–level information to a foreign entity. You understand me, Pyke? So help me, God, do not play with me."

Executed. A word I had not heard from them before. But with basic context, I could assume the General just threatened Pyke. Threatened him for disclosing information to me, about my species. What had they done? I don't have any more time. I must escape. The humans are turning out to be perhaps the most horrific creatures in the cosmos.

"Yes, sir, I was just—"

"Ramirez, babysit the doctor. He doesn't leave your sight. Understood?" The General had a habit of interrupting Pyke.

"Yes, sir." Ramirez raised an extremity to meet his head just above one of his visual organs as he responded.

However unlikely, I could not underestimate the humans again. They could have found my world, and based on how I'd been treated, that could only mean catastrophic consequences awaited my species. There had never been a galaxy-traveling species as primitive and archaic as the humans. My kind would have no reason to expect violence, of all things. I had to get out. I had to warn my race of this impending doom. But my body was growing weak. The reproduction of a new body to transfer my consciousness into costs energy and precious resources.

Pyke had been watching me for weeks now. My every move, my every internal thought had been done under the presence of his eyes. Undoubtedly, the growth on my underside had caught his attention, and my lethargic mannerisms hadn't gone unnoticed.

"What's happening to it, Doc?" Ramirez inquired, peering in at me curiously.

"A new body. It's creating a new form. The same way our cells divide and reproduce, so do they. Except much more advanced. They produce an entire new self and transfer consciousness into it. At least that's my theory."

Pyke's theory was correct, of course.

"A new body? So they just don't die?" The thought of prolonged life clearly interested Ramirez, leading me to the assumption that humans may have short life spans.

"I can't say for certain. It's more than likely not an infinite cycle. But it's certainly possible that without being killed, they could potentially repeat this process indefinitely. I'm only just now learning how often they must generate a new frame to inhabit."

Pyke was indeed getting more information about me. I wasn't feigning my loss of strength. So much focus is put into constructing a new form.

"Scary stuff." Ramirez stated.

It would appear that humans fear what they don't understand. There would be no reason to feel fear or anxiety about my life cycle.

"Scary but lucky. This might be the only chance we'll get to move it. They go unconscious for a period after the transfer of consciousness. For how long, I'm not sure. Even if it wakes up, though, it's small enough to control for a time being."

Pyke was correct again. When I transfer my mind, everything fades briefly due to the physical strain of it all. This would be the moment the humans had been waiting for.

"How long until it happens?"

Ramirez's question was answered by the sound of my body collapsing to the ground. My smaller newly formed corpse detaching and sprawling out.

"Astonishing. It created an entire new self in less than forty-eight hours." Pyke pressed his hands to the glass, staring in with the same awe he once had for me. "Prepare for subject retrieval."

Ramirez donned a full body-encompassing suit to protect him from whatever bacteria or diseases they feared I carried. Pyke did the same.

"Opening subject access gate 1." The voice was muffled, but I could tell it was Pyke.

The wall that had entrapped me on my first escape attempt parted in the middle. Due to the confined space, my larger body lay almost directly next to it. Pyke and Ramirez carefully stepped over my fallen corpse, Ramirez holding some sort of tool requiring both extremities to hold its weight. It was a long thin object that he kept directed at my larger motionless body. The humans leaned down toward my small lifeless reproduction as Pyke put some sort of bindings on all four limbs.

Pyke jolted and planted his backside against the far wall that had not been opened, dropping my small lure in the process. Surely, upon hearing the sound of Ramirez's screams, Pyke knew he had made a miscalculation. The snapping and crunching of the inner framework holding Ramirez together made Pyke cry out in horror, surely understanding he would be next if I so chose.

I released what was once Ramirez to the floor, the sound being more akin to liquid spilling than a solid dropping, as I'd crushed nearly everything solid in his anatomy.

"Please, please, please, please, please!" Pyke shouted while looking away, perhaps not wanting to see his own kind dismembered.

"You made a critical assumption, among many others, Pyke."

Pyke seared his eyes into me, towering before him.

"H-h-how … how do … how do you …" Pyke's words came out in intervals with his exhalation of whatever chemical humans used to sustain their function.

"I can create new forms at will. Whether or not I choose to transition my consciousness into said forms is also at my discretion." The actual sound of my vocalization was clearly jarring to Pyke as well. I emitted noises that were unlike anything made by a human.

"I'm sorry, I'm sorry. I didn't mean to. I never knew what they'd do," Pyke begged not to be eviscerated without directly saying so.

Lifting Pyke off his feet caused an instant audible reaction.

"No, no, no, please, I can help you escape!" Pyke pleaded in an attempt to bargain.

I was just inches from the scientist, holding him at my mercy. No glass, no walls. Just us two intellects—reduced to savages. Killing, and begging not to be killed.

"What has come of my world? My species, have you found them?" My line of questioning would be direct. Surely, others would arrive soon to subdue me.

"The military. The military traced where we found you back to the closest habitable world." Pyke stuttered.

"What has come of my world? Answer." Pyke had perhaps misheard me as he had replied to only half of my question.

"They made contact. Two days later, an orbital nuclear strike was ordered. Your species was deemed a threat, and your world was habitable for humans."

"What does that mean, Pyke? Nuclear strike. Are you implying a destruction of atoms on my origin world?" *What have they done?* I thought. My species would never just attack a visiting race on our world. Why would the humans engage in violence with no apparent provocation?

"Nuclear weapons. We made them. Humans I mean. We made them almost a thousand years ago. The weapon splits atoms and causes catastrophic damage. It will be decades before humans can inhabit your world now, but it's how humans have survived for centuries."

An emotion my kind is so unfamiliar with: sorrow. We know of it, we have felt it; but in our countless years, we have so rarely felt. I felt it then, more than ever. More than I ever even knew possible.

"Extermination? My species was annihilated so yours may inhabit my world for generations to come?" Though the horrendous sorrow was overbearing, I could not understand why Pyke would admit this to me. Clearly his species is familiar with the concept of vengeance. Additionally, it must be clear that while in my very grasp, this information could be deadly to Pyke.

"I never wanted any of this. I just wanted to learn. I didn't know what they were going to do. I didn't even know we found your world until two days after I discovered you were sentient. I thought you were an animal."

"Animal?" I began to respond. "You thought I, the one captured and maimed, to be the animal? Perhaps if your species spent as much time analyzing alternative energy sources as you did world-destroying weapons, you wouldn't need to kill entire races for your own survival. And perhaps if you'd just asked us, we could have shared our eons of knowledge with you."

I was then interrupted by a light thud from behind my visual scope. Repeated, but faint. I turned to see the source of this annoyance, only to find more humans, holding the same tools that Ramirez had wielded. The tools were launching some sort of small projectile at me. My outer layer was far too durable for this to do anything of notice, but clearly, this was meant to harm me, perhaps even kill me. I released Pyke for a brief moment to dismember my would-be killers. They cried out shrieks of pain, each and every one of them. Twisting and snapping, crunching and crushing. Then it was only Pyke and me again. I turned toward the cowering survivor of my onslaught, towering over him so I may tell him his species' error.

"I have never built an object with the intention to harm another life-form. Nor have my people. We create to grow. We create to learn. But now you have destroyed endless eternities of knowledge—the information my kind has gathered over eons of existing and studying the cosmos and all its workings. As you have dragged me down to your barbaric primal ways here, your species has done so infinite times over with its destruction of my race. I will use my knowledge of this universe and its contents, and I too will build a weapon. Your kind is a disease on the endless. So to the endless I shall return you."

Those were the last words my dear Pyke heard before I removed his cognitive organ from the rest of his corpse. As I now stand atop my world-ending mechanism—a device that condenses matter until gravity itself pulls even light inward to an all-crushing hole of nothing—I float in the orbit of the humans' last remaining world. I saved this one for last, of course, out of sentiment. My origin world. Now crawling with an infestation of humans, I shall make one final use of my device. If only Pyke were here to see it.

NEMESIS

Like waking from a dream, George came to sprawled out on his kitchen floor. His clothes felt damp and heavy on him, as they shared the same crimson coat of plasma that his hands did.

"No, no, no," George exclaimed aloud. "Why? What is wrong with you?"

George began to climb the kitchen counter to rise to his feet, but a sharp pain brought him plunging back to the floor. He grasped his abdomen, near his hip on the left side. That's where the source of the agony resided.

"What? What the hell did you do?" George asked.

"Oh, give me a break. It's the first time I've ever gotten caught." George spoke out loud to himself. His voice had a slight bit of rasp upon his self-appointed answer.

"Caught? What do you mean caught?"

"Not like that. I mean hit. They caught me with a knife."

George's dialogue with himself took place in an empty home aside from his own presence. He had lived alone in a small house in a suburban neighborhood. Yet he still found himself speaking nearly in a whisper. George scanned his body, disgusted by the galore of blood he was soaked in, and equally disturbed that this time, not all of it was foreign.

"You got me stabbed?" George lifted his shirt to see the repulsive wound. The flesh was twisted and mangled, blood still dripping from the gash.

"Us stabbed, George. I got us stabbed."

Contrary to his inner counterpart, George hated gore. Seeing his own flesh contorted and spewing blood reminded him of his mortality.

"Us? Us? There is no us." George slowly began to rise off the kitchen floor again, this time with more prudence due to his newfound woe.

"Can we not do this tonight, George? Really. Just for once."

"No. There is no us. There is you, and there is me. We aren't the same."

George got to his feet and then limped toward the sink. He wasn't much of a trauma expert, so giving care to this fresh laceration would prove perplexing. That being said, he had seen enough TV to know the basics, he'd thought.

Clean the wound, cover it up. That's first and foremost. A doctor's visit would have to wait. No way he could stumble into an emergency room right now, the night of a murder, and not instantly become a suspect for the heinous crime his peer had committed. Surely, whatever blade had been used to pierce his gut would be examined, and the difference in blood from the victim would be noticed. A report would be sent out to watch for an injured suspect. Wait a minute? George thought.

"You imbecile!"

"What?"

George looked frantic. He had one hand still clamped onto his bleeding fissure, the other was nervously gripping his scalp.

"You got me stabbed, and when the cops find the knife, they can link it to me! You're going to get me sent to prison!"

George's mouth began to let out a patronizing chuckle.

"What's so funny about this? My life is over! Do you know what that means for you too?"

"Calm down, George." The response came out just as condescending as the laughter. "I took care of all that. The knife is gone. Bitch got me good with it. I took care of her too."

"Stop." George blurted out in hopes of expelling any chance of hearing more details. Though, he knew better.

"C'mon, George. You know half the fun is filling you in on what you missed out on."

"You know how I feel about that. What you do is disgusting. I want no part in it."

"A part in it? George you are it. Your hands—my hands. They're the same, pal. You diced her up same as me."

"Enough!" George demanded. He turned on the sink and grabbed a rag off the kitchen counter and began running it through the flowing warm water. "Stop blaming me. Or trying to pull me down with you. You do what you do. No more making yourself feel better by pretending I'm as bad as you are."

George felt good about his response. Surely, that would shut him up, he thought. Now just to push this rag to the wound and, hopefully, stop it from getting infected before he could get real treatment. A dog bit him? No, it clearly wasn't a wound an animal would cause. An accident while doing yard work? Possibly. Maybe while trying to build a fence. That could work. Clumsily fell onto his shovel while digging holes for posts. A sharp shovel. Yes, that would do.

"You're the one pretending, George."

George sighed. He was almost certain he was done dealing with this for the night.

"What are you on about now?" He continued to press the warm rag to his side, doing his best not to look at the carnage so as to prevent vomiting.

"The girl tonight—she must'a been no more than seventeen. You know that?"

"I don't want to hear any of this."

"Listen, now." The voice was assertive, and strangely imposing for an exclamation coming from George's own mouth.

"She was just a kid. I knocked on the door asking for her dad. I watched her parents leave an hour before. Lucky for me, you look like a schoolyard bitch. So she didn't think twice about opening the door to talk with me."

"What are you getting at?"

"As soon as she opened the door, I threw myself into the house. I tried snagging the little shit, but she took off down the hall. I thought she was going for the phone. Sneaky little thing was going for the kitchen knife. I almost wanted to stop and admire her for that, to tell you the truth."

"Why are you telling me this? I don't care about the sick, twisted things you do. And I don't want to hear about them. Let me live my life in peace."

"You don't care I butchered that girl?"

"That's not what I meant." George had grown exhausted from the conversation, or perhaps the loss of blood. Maybe a bit of both. He began hunting through the kitchen cabinets for bandages. He knew he had kept them somewhere in here. He had to get this wound covered, anything to do that would keep his mind from visualizing too much of what he had been hearing.

"I'm not so sure about that, George. Because after that girl pushed that knife into us, I grabbed her. I got hold of her and gouged out her eyes."

"Enough!" George yelled as he slammed his fists into the kitchen counter with provoked rage. "It's enough I have to share my head with you, I will not sit here and listen to you gloat about your disgusting practices."

George had dealt with this time and time again. Time after time, he would awake with blood-soaked hands and a new confession to listen to. Always horrified by the vile acts themselves, and hearing the pleasure in his voice as the story was gleefully unfolded. But he had finally had enough. He could not bear it anymore. He would end this tonight, he told himself.

"I'm done hearing about all of this. I won't listen. I won't." George's lips pulled up into a smirk.

"You will."

He was losing his grip on reality. And sanity—however much of that he had left anyways. With all his sincerity, he meant what he'd said. He'd had enough of hearing about these atrocities. But really, what could he do? It was not like he could just not listen. They shared the same ears, mouth, and body. There was simply no way to avoid him. He would carry him everywhere he went the rest of his life, and be forced to hear all the grueling details of sadistic murder. He was at the mercy of his own voice.

"You will listen, George." The devilish smirk smeared across his face was still prominent. "After I was done with her eyes, I threw her to the floor. She was screaming so loud. I almost didn't want to cover her mouth. I knew I had to, of course. But God, I just wanted to sit there and listen to those screams. It just completed me. What I'd been searching for, for so long. The perfect screech of pain and fear. They were so magnificent. I was finally in the euphoria I'd longed for."

George had both his hands pressed tightly to his ears; he had to drown out the noise. Anything to stop this tormenting tale.

"George," he heard the voice. But this—this was … different. "George, you can't drown me out. We are legion."

George's skin grew hot, and the hairs on his arms shot up like a spring flower. Why could he hear the voice in his own thoughts?

"I climbed on top of her. I pushed my hand over her mouth so tight I think I broke her jaw. I brought our knife, but the one she got me with—it just seemed equitable I gut her with it."

"Please!" George cried aloud. "Please. No more. No more." Tears rolled down his cheeks. The thought of his body, his hands performing these acts, against his will or not, appalled him.

"George, I disemboweled that little girl. She's not the first. She won't be the last. And you're my colleague. My willing participant."

"No!" George would not stand for this. "That's a lie! You know that's a lie!"

"Is it George?" the voice in George's head questioned, in a tone that sounded of genuine curiosity. "You've stood by for years. Almost a decade. We have eviscerated more than a dozen people. You could stop me, if you really wanted to."

George knew what he was trying to do. But it wouldn't work. He would not let him. George knew he had nothing to do with these murders. Besides the obvious use of his body, his consciousness never committed these crimes.

"There's nothing I can do about it. I lose time. Then I come back, and you have done terrible things. Not me."

"C'mon, George. Be a little more creative. How could you stop me? If you really wanted to?"

This thought had never really occurred to George. Well, he couldn't call the police … surely, they would not believe him, that his body killed those people, but without him at the helm. Suicide? That's not an option. Thanatophobia had plagued George since he was a boy, when his father first told him, "Everybody dies one day, son." So what is it? How could he stop him? No solution seemed viable.

"Both of those options would work." The voice came to George once more.

"What? What do you mean? How do you…?"

"George, I know everything you're thinking. You tell yourself I'm a different person living in your body. I'm not. I'm you, George. I am George."

"Liar!" Even the thought of accepting what he'd just heard repulsed him. *It's lies. It's slander. It's deception. He just wants to make me squirm,* George thought.

"I'm nothing like you. I'm a good person."

Maniacal laughter erupted in George's head.

"Sure we are, George. You've only flayed a few people."

"No, no, no, you did that, not me."

"We did it, George. I am you. You are me. And if you truly are a good person, you'd have stopped yourself from having these outbursts a long time ago."

George could barely respond now through his sobs. His words came out in barely a whimper. "I never did anything. I didn't hurt anybody."

"Try telling them that." The voice snickered.

Wait. What had he said? George postured up. "Tell who, what?" What was he getting at here?

"George, I'd told you. I found my euphoria. I'm completed, so to speak."

"Tell who, what?" George repeated.

The voice in George's head let out a long sigh.

"Well, George, I never took care of that knife. Matter of fact, I called the police. Gave'm the address too."

"What address?" George shouted frantically.

"Our address, of course."

George's gaze ricocheted across the room as he thought about his options in panic. But surely this was a joke? A cruel ploy to get a rise out of him, right? As the voice had been telling him, they were one. They were bound together. Surely he didn't want to spend the rest of his life in prison?

"It's not a joke, George. Killing that girl tonight completed me. I'm finally at peace. Now I just want to sit back and watch you squirm for a couple years."

George was lost, his mind cluttered with thoughts, shooting from one to the next so quickly he couldn't make sense of anything.

"What do you mean? You'll be in prison too? And a couple of years? We'll be in prison for life!" George shouted.

"I've always been in a prison," the voice replied solemnly. "You only let me out when your head can't handle the world anymore. But I've finally found my peace. Now I can just sit back and watch the show."

This was absurd. He couldn't mean this. There was no way this was anything but an act to upset him, George thought.

"And it won't be for life. We got the death penalty in this state, ol' George. I'll be watching you panic all the way up until the bitter end."

No. No this simply cannot be happening. George could not process all this at once. The wound, the story about the girl, and now what this voice was telling him. That he would be locked up and await death. Death. A thought that lingered with him day and night. A thought that terrified him. The finality of it. The nothingness of it. The void. His nervous banter in his head was interrupted by the sound of sirens. No. No, he couldn't have.

"You idiot! If they kill me, you'll die too!"

More of the same condescending laughter came pouring out of George's mouth.

"You think I haven't thought of that? I don't care. It'll be worth watching you rip yourself apart from the inside. It's the one kind of fear I never get to see when I'm out. I never get to see the best kind. The kind you manifest in your own thoughts. The kind only a mind's privacy can conjure."

The sound of car doors slamming shut and sirens just outside the house confirmed the voice's story. He had told the truth.

"George Moore, open up, it's the police," a loud declaration accompanied by pounding on his front door jolted George.

This was it. In the back of his mind, he knew this day would come, but always buried it. Always denied it.

"And one more thing George," the voice said aloud.

The police had been knocking for thirty seconds or so. They clearly were not feeling patient, given the gruesome nature of the crime they were responding to. The front door was kicked in, and a brigade of officers stormed into the house. They found George on his knees in the kitchen, still stained with the blood of the young girl and the puncture wound she had given him.

"I've always been you."

J -4

No. *There's no way this is happening*, I said to myself as the correctional officer escorted me down the bleak long hallway. The walls were painted a baby blue, with white accents. Apparently, this color combination was meant to be soothing. Whichever psychologist formed that theory had clearly never been locked up. No colors or patterns could ease your suffering in this place.

"Open J Block. Inmate Switzer returning."

The officer grunted as he gripped the radio on his shoulder. A loud clacking sound marked the unlocking of the large metal door before me, with an all-too-familiar black J painted on it. Home sweet home. I reached out my hands to be released from my handcuffs before I reentered the cell block. This routine was my life. Never leaving the block without restraints. Like I was an animal. Upon reentry into the block, the wave of orange suited men crowded me.

"What's the deal?"

"How many years?"

"Are you getting out?"

Everyone with questions. Each one of them, of course, posed as though they truly cared about my outcome. I knew better. This place was empty. The only thing passing the time is hearing the latest news.

"Who is getting out?"

"Who is serving life?"

"Who jumped who?" That's all it was. They needed fresh information to satisfy their frenzied need to be included.

"Fifteen." I answered the mob, doing my best to seem unwavering.

"Fifteen?" one of the men in the crowd called out. "That's insane man. You didn't even pull the trigger."

I knew everything they were about to say to me. Attempts to comfort. Some sort of tribalism, I suppose. We were all inmates, so feeling frustrated on my behalf, I presumed, made them feel like good people. But I knew the truth. J Block was not for the good people. Everyone in here had either killed or had assisted someone who killed. We were not good people, but regardless of that, I never killed anyone. I was lumped in with the murderers. The guards, the judge, everyone saw me the same way they saw these men. Another killer.

I had to hold back tears. This was not a place to cry, but the idea of my wife and children seeing me the same way that everyone else did now was gutting me. I told the others I was tired after a long day. It's not completely a lie. I am exhausted, but I more just seek refuge from there prowling eyes, so I can suffer in silence and peace. I entered my cell, J-4. My home for the last Sixteen months. My cell buddy is laid out on his bunk, his jumpsuit on the floor. The cell was the only place you were allowed to take it off. He was wearing old torn-up shorts and a sleeveless white shirt that was as dirty as the shorts were torn.

"I overheard the news. Fifteen years. Man, I'm sorry." His remark seemed genuine, surprisingly. I'd only known him for about four weeks. He had been brought in from another facility and had been bunking with me ever since.

"Thanks, Blankenship." I replied as I retired to my bunk. We all went by last names here. The officers called us by our last names, and it just kind of stuck with us.

"Ya know. I got hung up on the same thing." Blankenship began to say as he sat up on his bunk.

Strangely enough, I never asked him what he was in for. That's usually the first bit of conversation in here. But we were both quiet guys, Blankenship and I. So it never really came up. We never really talked at all, which made this a strange but welcome shift.

"I was mugging someone with my buddy. It wasn't the first time. But buddy got spooked. Ended up shooting the guy. Got me twenty five."

"Shit," I responded. "Makes me feel lucky for fifteen," I joked. "I was robbing a gas station of all things. Stupid. I made fine money at my job. But my buddy talked me into it." The story hurt to tell because every time I thought of that moment, I was reminded of how easily I could have just said no, and I would never have been here. "Next thing I know, my friend is shooting the cashier. Claims he saw the guy reaching for a gun." What hurts even more is the hindsight knowledge that the cashier had no gun. Just a scared minimum wage worker, shot and killed for no better reason.

"What are the odds, right?" Blankenship said with a sigh. "Same boat brought us to the same island."

"Yeah, no kidding." Though the pain of my verdict was still settling in, it was comforting to hear someone else with such a similar dilemma.

"Now my wife, my kids. They all have to go fifteen years without me. My boys will be adults by the time I'm out."

I could feel my throat swell up, and my eyes followed shortly after as I did everything in my power to not sob.

"You from around here, Switzer?"

I wasn't sure if Blankenship was genuinely curious, or if he noticed my dismay and was just clearing the air. Regardless, I did not mind the change of subject.

"Yes, I am. Been here all my life." I was able to get a hold of my emotions rather quickly, and the swelling in my eyes and throat were diminishing.

"That's cool, man. I've never been here, ya know, besides this place anyways. They sent me here so I wouldn't be in the same jail as my codefendant before getting sent off to state."

That was very common. It was the reason my friend who shot that cashier was in the jail the next county over.

"Yeah, it's a nice town, outside of this shithole, anyways. I still live on the same road I grew up on. Dalton Road, house has a big red door and a picket fence. It's like the American dream, ya know." I laughed a little while saying this, given my current predicament.

"That sounds nice, man. Real nice. With a wife and some kids. Sounds like you had it made."

"Yeah, I really did."

Opening up to cell buddies I'd met a few weeks ago was not a habit of mine, but after the events of the day, I was particularly vulnerable. Just talking to someone who understood my situation was soothing. I was not one of the other inmates. They were killers. They didn't understand what it was like for me. Or for Blankenship. Someone in here, grouped up with the others and labeled a killer when I had never hurt a soul. Not the guards, because they too looked at people like me and Blankenship with judgment, as if we were the same as the killers we lived in J block with.

But finally, here was someone who truly understood.

"Hey man, I know this is gonna sound crazy, but hear me out."

I was intrigued. "Yeah, what's up?"

Whatever he was going to say couldn't hurt me to at least listen, I thought.

"This is just a county lockup. The security here ain't no state penitentiary." Blankenship's voice bordered on a whisper as he glanced toward the cell door as if to confirm no one was watching, or listening. "If we ever wanted to get out, this would be the place to do it. Not a prison. We'd have to do it before we got sent out."

"What?" I responded, my tone clearly conveying the absurdity of his remarks. "Like a prison break? You wanna try and break out?"

What a romantic idea. To simply escape. And to have said it as if it were so simple. I almost wanted to laugh.

"I know. I know. It sounds …" He paused for a moment, his eyes roaming all over the room as if he was searching for the right words before continuing. "Impractical. But listen. I know how these facilities work. And this place ain't that big. We'll need to get one guard's uniform, pick a night they got a rookie in the control room. And we're out of here."

I was genuinely flabbergasted.

"One guard's uniform? Are you nuts? How the hell are we gonna pull that one off?" I continued to rant in a whispered scream. "And a rookie in the control room? You think 'cause he's a rookie he's dumb enough to just open all the doors for us?"

Though I was being very harsh, Blankenship did not seem offended. If anything, he appeared encouraged to try harder to convince me.

"The uniform won't be hard. Look, I'm not saying we really hurt anyone bad, but we'd just have to hit the guy over the head when he comes in to inspect our room. That's all."

"Hit him over the head?" My expression was one of bewilderment. "You want us to attack a CO? And what, add ten more years to my time?"

"It's not like that" he was quick to assure me. "We pick our target. Someone around my size. There are two of us and no cameras in the cells. He comes in, one of us grabs him, one of us hits him. I've only been here a few weeks, and if we got a newbie in the control room, he won't recognize me as an inmate, and he more than likely won't know every officer's face yet either. We just go over the radio and tell him to open the doors, and it will look like I'm an officer escorting you through the jail. It's simple."

"Simple? The whole plan involves assuming someone won't recognize you, and that we somehow will know who is working the control room. That's insane." I was far less than convinced. There was no way I was doing something so reckless just to get ten more years. Or who knows, maybe even more. I wasn't sure what they gave guys who attack officers, or attempt impossible prison breaks, for that matter.

"We'll know 'cause we'll ask." Blankenship was persistent. "These officers are local county kids. A lot of them are nineteen or twenty. We just ask them who is working control. They will answer without thinking twice."

He was right about one thing. Most of the officers in this jail were young guys. Young guys fresh out of high school just trying to make some money, or looking to jump over to the police side once they were of age.

"We ask who's working control, we wait till it's a night where we get a newer guy. We get the guards uniform who's doing cell checks. Go up to control, tell him to let us in. He unlocks the door, we go in. Rough him up a little, use the control monitor to open the front doors, and we're out of here. We just have to do it right after they do their head count. That will give us a few hours before anyone realizes something's up."

Now I was almost angry. How stupid did he think I was?

"Rough him up? Do you hear yourself? Your plan requires us to assault two officers, then hope they stay unconscious until we're out the door and gone. Then what? Where do we go? What am I gonna do, go home and wait till they arrest me again?"

This was the most moronic idea I'd ever heard. Blankenship's imagination must be overwhelmingly strong to create such a picture-perfect plan that requires so many coincidences and random chance, yet he still seemed so confident in the idea.

"Look, Switzer. I didn't kill no one. You didn't kill no one. It's not right that we should serve a quarter of our lives behind bars. I don't wanna hurt no one either. But if hitting a CO or two is the price for my freedom, I'll pay that." His confidence was still unwavering. "Do you really wanna miss your kids growing up?"

"Of course I don't. But where am I going to hide once I'm out? There's nowhere to go. I'd get sent right back here. There's just no way."

Blankenship looked to the floor. He seemed drained of his bravado as he sighed, letting out the last bit of hope he had.

"What if we all went to Europe?"

I was baffled. How could he even think to suggest that? "Europe? How the hell am I going to get to Europe?"

"I know a guy." A glimmer of gusto seemed to be coming back quickly with this new development in his plan. "We get out, go to your house, get your family, and we get out of the country. I know. I know. This sounds insane. It sounds impossible. But we can do it. This is county lock up. They don't know what to do with shit like this. We'd be gone before anyone knew what was going on."

"Yeah, sure, but then I have to go to Europe just to live? Take my kids from their home?" *Surely, this would end the debate,* I thought.

Blankenship leaned toward me as if to make sure I was paying close attention to his next remark.

"Your kids and your wife—I bet they'd rather live in Europe with their father and husband than live here without you. Those kids are gonna blame you. They'll hate you for not being around. So will your wife. Even though it's not your fault. You didn't hurt nobody. They deserve to grow up with their dad around. And you deserve to watch them grow up. Just think about it."

Fifteen years, I thought. Fifteen years in a prison. Fifteen years of shackles, like an animal. My kids would resent me. Blankenship was right. My wife, she might move on. No one can be expected to wait for fifteen years. I could lose my kids and the love of my life. Forever. But this? This plan? It was insane. It was impossible. But the more I thought about it, the more I considered it. It wasn't really that far-fetched. I've been escorted up and down these halls countless times. I know the layout like the back of my hand. Plus, the midnight shift had half the officers of the day shifts. If we got up the hall and in the control room, we would easily be able to pop the front door open.

"The front door automatically locks every time it shuts. And when control unlocks it, it only stays unlocked for about two seconds before locking up again. How do you plan on us unlocking it from control and getting out before it just locks up again?"

Blankenship grinned. He could tell by my question that I was starting to consider this farce.

"You will have to wait in control while I walk to the front door. I'll be in uniform, so no one should suspect anything if we play it cool. You watch the cameras, wait till you see me at the door, and pop it open. I'll open it and hold it while you run down from control. Then we're out."

This was insanity, but it started to become real in my head. The way he laid it out, it really seemed . . . possible.

"With six or so guards on the midnight shift, we'd have one down and out in our cell. One down and out in control. That leaves four other guys walking around this place. The odds we'd even bump into one of them is slim to none."

I could not believe what I was saying. But Blankenship had me sold. It was possible.

"I'm telling you, we can do it." Blankenship stated with conviction. I was all in. Screw wasting my life away in a prison. As crazy as a jail break was, as crazy as moving my entire family to Europe was, spending the next fifteen years inside a cell without my family seemed crazier. "Now we just wait for the right guy. We just need the right two officers working at midnight."

And wait we did. We needed a tall, lean officer working our block. But also one we were confident we could overpower. We also needed a rookie working control. So we waited. Each day I woke up with my stomach in a knot. Was this the day? I would ask myself. Every single morning, wondering if this was the day we would make our move. Day after day of feeling nervous to the point of nausea.

Then finally, two weeks later, the midnight shift was coming on, and we saw Officer Davis walk into the block. Davis was around six feet tall, and thin. Just the size that Blankenship could fit naturally into his uniform. On top of that, Davis had been working here less time than I'd been locked up. I remembered him coming on about six months ago. Young and anxious. Still a nervous rookie. Blankenship and I locked eyes. We knew the last piece of the puzzle we needed. We had other officers working our block on midnights who would have been perfect in the last two weeks as well, but each one of those nights, we regrettably learned that a veteran officer was working control. Would tonight be different? Was this the night we got out of here, the night we got our freedom back?

"How you doin', Davis?" Blankenship casually uttered to the patrolling officer.

"Doing all right, Blankenship." Officer Davis responded in his best attempt at a professional voice.

"Who y'all got working control tonight?" Blankenship continued to probe.

Davis stopped snooping around our cell for a moment to answer Blankenship's question. "Uhh … Gorman? I think."

Yes! I cried internally. This was it. Gorman started one month ago. She was the newest officer in the entire jail.

I jumped back, startled. Blankenship had viciously jolted at Davis in a frenzy, striking him in the jaw. The thud of his fist slamming into the officer's jaw made me wince, and the cracks I'd heard surely implied he'd broken Davis's jaw on contact.

What the hell? Blankenship took less than two seconds to ferociously assault Officer Davis upon hearing Gorman's name. I didn't know what to do. I panicked.

Davis was on the ground, whimpering, clearly still conscious, but also too injured to cry out, as Blankenship rained down blow after blow on his head. I could hear Davis spitting and gurgling blood. Blankenship was raising his raw bleeding knuckles to deliver what must have been the twentieth punch, when I called out to intervene.

"Blankenship!" I was attempting to yell, but under my breath so we might still go unnoticed. "What the hell are you doing?"

Blankenship whipped his head around and glared at me, a crazed look in his eyes.

"Do you wanna get out of here or not?" he growled, still holding Davis's throat with one hand with the other hand raised, ready to deliver the next blow.

"Pl-plea … ," Davis began to whimper, coughing out blood between syllables.

No, why did you do that? I said to myself. *Davis, you poor fool. Why did you speak up?* Clearly, Blankenship had an appetite for violence, and Davis's words implied consciousness. I knew this would be all the invitation Blankenship would need to continue with his savagery.

"Shut your mouth," Blankenship snarled as he cracked his knuckles into Davis' mouth repeatedly.

Finally, Davis stopped moving. Blankenship jumped to his feet. "All right, help me get the clothes off him, Switzer."

Davis was lying there motionless in a small pool of his blood. Teeth were scattered on the floor around his head, and his eyes were swollen shut. His face had been bashed in, to the point where he wasn't recognizable. Battered and discolored, contorted to the point of seeming inhuman. *What have we done?* Now I had no choice. Just like before. Just like with my friend at the gas station. Now I had to get out, or what had been done to this man would be done to me.

"Switzer, get your ass over here and help me get this dude's clothes off!" Blankenship hissed.

I rushed over, pulling the uniform off Davis's broken body. Blankenship threw his jumpsuit off and quickly began suiting up in the CO's uniform.

"All right, let's go," Blankenship said, walking confidently out of the cell. I followed, taking one last look at Officer Davis before I stumbled out.

Blankenship grasped the radio on the shoulder of his newly acquired uniform and pressed the button to open the line.

"Control, open J block."

The moment of truth. I was sweating through my jumpsuit while I clenched my jaw tight enough that I might have broken some of my teeth. My heart felt heavier, like it could sink right down through my stomach. Then the sound of that familiar clack. The door had been unlocked. Relief rushed through me as I took a long deep breath in. We made it out.

But my relief was short-lived.

"C'mon, Switzer, let's go," Blankenship said as he began up the hall.

Gorman was a small girl, barely out of high school. She looked like she weighed no more than a buck fifteen. What would Blankenship do to her when we got to control?

"Blankenship."

"Shut up, Switzer," he snapped at me. "We don't want to bring any attention to us. Be quiet."

I chose to ignore him. "Gorman is just a kid. Don't go so hard on her, all right, man?"

"Switzer, keep your mouth shut. You didn't help with Davis. It's clear if we're gonna get out, it will be because of me, so we're doing it my way."

What did I get myself into? We were approaching the control room. Blankenship pulled me off to the side of the hall.

"If she sees you in your jumpsuit, she won't let me in. Not even rookies are gonna let an inmate, even a supervised one, into control. Wait right here. I'll go in. Count to sixty, then come to the door and I'll let you in."

"Al-alright," I stuttered.

Blankenship zipped away toward the control room door. I heard his voice softly from a distance. "Control, let me in. I left something in there last shift."

Then the clack of the door unlocking. Blankenship whipped the door open and walked in. The glass to the control room was thick. I couldn't hear exactly what was going on. But I counted to sixty like instructed.

I began moving toward the door, terrified to go in and see what he had done to that girl. I gripped the door handle and waited for Blankenship to unlock it. As the lock came open, I pulled the large metal door back and then peered inside. I looked on in horror at what I saw.

Gorman was sprawled out lying face down in a massive pool of blood. Her blonde hair was completely soaked in a coat of crimson. The stillness of her body drove me insane in mere moments. It was almost as though her body's motionlessness could speak, telling me the story of pain she'd endured, or failed to endure.

"Blankenship, what did you do?" I cried out, tears ripping down my face. This young girl had to be dead. The blood had now seeped all the way from her body to the door, pooling around my shoes.

"I couldn't risk her waking up and calling the cops, man."

"You never said we were going to kill anyone!" My throat was tight, but I shouted as best I could through my sobs. "What the hell is wrong with you? You're sick. You're disgusting!"

"Forget about her, Switzer. We're almost out. I'm going to the front door. Buzz it open, I'll hold it and wait for you to run down. Then we're gone."

Blankenship clicked the unlock button on the control monitor for the door leading to the hallway and then stormed out.

I was trying to watch the security cameras to see when he got to the front door. My attempts to hold back vomit were worthless. I threw up all over the control room desk. This girl was dead on the floor. And I helped him do it.

My guilty thoughts were interrupted when I saw Blankenship by the front door on the camera, waving back and forth to get my attention.

Do I open this door? Do I let this monster go? If I don't I'm trapped here too. If I don't let this animal out of its cage. I'll be charged with another murder. Maybe even two. Officer Davis could very well be dead… I've come this far. I can't take the fall for two more murders. I have to go home to my family.

While still weeping, I reached toward the control monitor and clicked on the front door's unlock button. Then I began to click the unlock button for the control room door. Time to go.

Wait. Wait no. What is he doing? I glanced back at the front door camera. Blankenship was gone. No. No this can't be right? He left me. No this is not happening. I looked at the cameras that were focused on the parking lot. There he was, sprinting away. Running out into the night. This can't be happening. God no this is not happening. I looked down at the lifeless body of the young girl on the floor.

What have I done … I sank to the floor. I buried my face in my folded arms, my crying now hysterical. More people were hurt because of me. More people were dead because of me. And now I would never get out of here. I would spend the rest of my life behind walls. I sat there crying. Waiting. Waiting to get caught. Every single minute passed by with grueling anticipation. I just wanted to get it over with. I couldn't bear seeing Gorman anymore, but I was too much of a coward to make myself known. Out of fear of what they would do to me. So I sat there. I sat there for an hour … maybe two … I couldn't tell anymore.

Suddenly I heard yelling. I raised my head up out of my arms to see two officers passing by. They quickly noticed me in my orange jumpsuit sitting and sobbing in the control room. They began screaming signal codes into their radios. The sergeant on duty came sprinting down the hall, keys in hand. They were to manually unlock the control door.

The door was flung open, and the sergeant and two officers who'd spotted me came flying in. They saw the body on the floor and clearly assumed it was my doing. The rule book went out the window. A furious barrage of fists came down on me, strike after strike. I was balled up on the floor, with my hands folded over my head in an ill-conceived attempt to protect myself.

"You piece of shit, what did you do!" one of the officers cried. The beating continued.

"What did you do!"

I could feel a couple of my ribs snap as an officer's boot crashed into my side.

"It wasn't me," I whimpered. "It wasn't … me."

"Oh yeah? Then who was it?" the officer screamed back in response with heated rage in his eyes. "Blankenship. It was Blankenship."

The beating stopped.

"Where is he now? Where is Blankenship?"

"He left me … he … left me," I was able to mumble. Speaking became difficult as my mouth was full of blood and breathing was labored due to my broken rib cage.

"Blankenship is gone?" the officer yelled as he grabbed the collar of my jumpsuit, pulling me to my knees.

"Ye-yes. He's gone." Blood trickled from my mouth as I spoke.

"Why would you help a sick freak like Blankenship get out? What the hell is wrong with you?" The officers were still in the grip of a blood-induced rage, but they had tears rolling down their cheeks as well as the realization set in that Gorman was dead.

"He said he was in for the same thing as me." Every word, every breath seemed more and more difficult.

"Blankenship was in for child murder and rape. He was going to the state penitentiary for life in one month. And you let him go."

My eyes grew wide. No … no, that can't be true. No, that's not possible. That cannot be true. Then a realization sank in. I lunged forward grabbing on to the officer. He quickly threw me to the ground and drove his knee into my back.

"Stop resisting!" He put his handcuffs on me as tightly as possible without crushing my wrists.

"Please. Please!" I begged as they handcuffed me. "I told him where I lived. "My wife and my boys are there alone. Please! You have to check on them!"

"We'll call that in after Gorman's body gets taken out of here and cleaned up. You disgusting waste. You're lucky we don't take you out back and put a bullet in you."

"Please, no, you have to check on them please!" I was frantically screaming. I had seen firsthand what Blankenship was capable of, and I told him right where my family was.

Now I sit in solitary. It has been another year here at the county jail. I had to go back to court. Charged with another murder. The murder of Officer Kaitlyn Gorman, as well as the attempted murder of Officer Ryan Davis. Davis had pulled through but had to retire from the jail. He made enough money from the jail, I'm sure he'll be fine the rest of his life. Apparently, they pay you if you get injured on the job. Go figure. The cops got to my house too late. They spared me the details, but apparently, they got there too late. No one has ever found Blankenship either. I still go back in my head to that moment. That moment that I opened that door for him. I was so scared I would spend the rest of my life behind bars and never see my family again. I still go back to that moment.

It Lurks in the Nothing

They looked on in horror at Dr. Robert Gordon's tortured flesh. Most of all, Dr. Elizabeth Gordon was in agony at the sight of this mangled monstrosity of meat and bone. To every other bystander, this was an impossible image. A man missing large amounts of contractile tissue, his skin drooping from the gashes where snapped bones protruded. How he was standing, much less walking, seemed a conundrum. To Elizabeth, however, that man was not a broken and lacerated living corpse. He was her husband.

The anomaly first appeared ten years prior. Its sudden appearance, bursting out of the void, captured the imagination, and the fear, of the entire world. The first week of its existence, it was surrounded by United States military forces. It was a spherical black object, stagnantly floating in the middle of a small town in Missouri. Roughly twelve feet in circumference, the object wasn't exceedingly large. Regardless, its instantaneous materialization was cause for concern.

Theories began sprouting from every corner of humanity. Perhaps a weapon from a foreign superpower. Some believed it to be alien. Other more radical members of society claimed it was the devil. Soon, though, Dr. Robert Gordon and Dr. Elizabeth Myers would be assigned the task of uncovering the anomaly's true nature.

One month after the anomaly first appeared, an entire outpost had been built around it, with the black floating orb being the nucleus of the base. The military would run this installation under the advisory of Dr. Gordon and Dr. Myers. Tests and inspections of the sphere started out as conservative as possible. Without knowing the true nature of the object, there was no telling what toying with it might do.

As human nature would have it, though, within one hundred days of the anomaly's appearance, a drone was flown into the black mass. To no one's surprise, all control and visual feeds from the drone instantly cut off upon entering the sphere. It would be the first of many drones sent into the anomaly, all meeting the same fate. Dr. Gordon theorized that inside was a warped dimension of some kind.

Dr. Gordon and Dr. Myers had not met before this assignment, but sharing this radical unprecedented assignment quickly forged a bond between them. Both young. Both passionate about their work. Both thrown into something they couldn't possibly understand yet expected to have all the answers. They understood each other. They relied on each other. The two would fall in love before either would dare to admit, until, finally, Dr. Gordon mustered the courage to ask Dr. Myers if she would like to spend time together outside of work. Gordon's attempt at courtship displayed his lack of experience in the matter, but Elizabeth found him more endearing for it. Two lonely scientists spending every waking hour working together, with the same interests and the same goals. It was only a matter of time. Dr. Elizabeth Myers became Dr. Elizabeth Gordon three years after starting her assignment with Robert. The two would solve all the anomaly's mysteries together.

The day the world was put on course toward its destruction started like any other day. After all these years, the anomaly was no longer viewed as a threat. Most of the world forgot about its existence and had moved on to the next big news. The black sphere that materialized in an instant, containing uncharted vistas unseen by man, had been forgotten by the masses. Until the four-year mark to the day of its appearance. On that day, Dr. Robert Gordon embarked on a foredoomed journey. After months of careful planning and risk assessment, Robert came to the conclusion that the only way to discover what lay beyond the black was to travel there himself. The obvious risks were abundantly clear to him, of course. This could mean instantaneous death. However, the risk was indeed calculated. Cameras had probed into the sphere via extended poles attached to drones, the idea being to partially enter the anomaly, just enough to record what was on the other side. Like placing your face underwater with a pair of goggles on, just enough to see beneath the sea's surface of lifelessness to reveal the bustling ocean floor. This didn't work, as the cameras were unable to record anything once it had penetrated the anomaly, but it did prove that simply entering the sphere did not mean instant destruction. This was enough for Robert. Elizabeth pleaded with her husband to abandon this lunacy, as she was sure that the risk far outweighed the reward.

"In the name of science, my love." He would say before kissing her forehead. This was Robert's easy cop-out to actually defending his argument for what was clearly a vastly underprepared expedition into what could be suicide. But it wasn't necessarily a lie. Truly, Robert was intent on entering this object in the name of discovery. All other efforts for the last four years had been entirely fruitless. This would be his moon landing. The moment that etched his name into textbooks for the rest of humankind's existence on this rock floating in the expanse. For all the good intentions Robert had, his desire to be recognized as a man of science would have consequences unfathomable to all living organisms on earth.

Wearing a protective hazmat suit, fitted with an oxygen tank to replenish clean air for two hours, and a belt holding a few pouches and tools, Robert walked toward the anomaly. "You come back in one piece." Elizabeth unfortunately said to her husband through the earpiece beneath his helmet.

"I will, baby." He unfortunately responded, before stepping forward and being swallowed by the blackness of the sphere. And that was the last time Dr. Robert Gordon would be seen for six years. Like the drones before him, but this time with much more sorrow, and regret, he was gone with no trace. Everyone mourned the loss, but Elizabeth felt the guilt in the most intimate way possible. All findings of every test or study on the anomaly would suggest that Robert's return had next-to-zero chance. She felt the guilt of letting her husband's zealous excitement infect her and allow her to throw all rational thought out the window. Elizabeth would question every last decision, down to whether or not her loving Robert was in itself his death sentence.

Had I not loved him, she thought, I would have seen things more clearly. Never allowed him to take such a bold risk. I let my judgment be clouded because I wanted to believe him so badly. I wanted to believe in him so badly. To support him. I killed him.

The guilt was enough to damn Elizabeth to six years of waiting. The rest of the world had a funeral, Elizabeth had a lighthouse. She would wait there, and like a ship lost at sea, one day Robert would see her light and follow it home. That was the story she told herself. Refusing to step away from the assignment, Elizabeth stayed and monitored the anomaly, waiting for it to spit her husband back out one day. She stood by and told herself that she would be his lighthouse and guide him home.

Now six years later, as Robert stumbled out from the treacherous black hole that had engulfed him for so long, Elizabeth got what she had been hoping for, but with terrible stipulations. Running out of her monitoring station overlooking the anomaly, she tried to get to her long-lost husband before he collapsed. There was so much to be said, from both of them, she knew. But the wounds proved damning to that end, as Robert's body lay dead in a pile of contorted meat by the time Elizabeth had gotten outside to embrace him.

Elizabeth dropped to her knees before the mound of gore, weeping to it as if her husband was still somewhere in all that blood and bone. She was not given long to mourn her husband's death for the second time, as the ramifications of his trip into the anomaly had followed him out. Gunfire alerted her to the situation as the screams beforehand, she assumed, were still from disgust and horror at the sight of her husband torn to pieces, walking about like a zombie. Looking up from her hands, where she'd buried her sobbing eyes, Elizabeth witnessed what she could only assume was the perpetrator of this vile act on her beloved Robert. A bipedal creature, standing tall despite its leaning forward on a top-heavy frame. Thin legs with jagged hooks where humans would find toes supported the thing, and its abdomen followed in proportion to its thin legs. The chest was broad, with a protruding breastplate. The arms, if you could call them that, were more like the legs of a crustacean and were the most outwardly alarming part of the creature's anatomy, as it had six of them, all ending with broad spearing tips. Where a head would be, there was instead a vascular pulsing membrane. This thing that was lurking in the anomaly, with such a grotesque image, let out a high-pitched chirp that would be expected from such a monster, but its next vocalization was the polar opposite to all previous assumptions of it. With gunfire ricocheting off its bare skin, it spoke.

"A species such as yours cannot be allowed to tamper with forces such as this."

Elizabeth had no time to process the happenings of the last minute. Her presumed-dead husband's return, him dying in front of her, the revelation of the creature that presumably killed him, then the use of the English language by the monstrous beast from the void. But before any more time was allotted to attempt rationalizing these events, the membrane on the creature's head began to split, and from it spewed a yellow gaseous cloud, spouting thirty feet into the air before dispersing beyond what human eyes can detect.

"What's it doing?" one of the soldiers shouted, still firing recklessly. The volume of bullets being volleyed at the life-form made his question rhetorical at best, as no one was able to hear it.

A few well-placed shots into the open orifice spewing the yellow gas seemed to rupture something vital, as it ceased spraying its yellow smog, then crumpled. Upon closer examination, they could see the visitor from the anomaly was indeed dead.

Dr. Elizabeth Gordon did try to save the world. She adamantly insisted that all individuals present for the creature's gaseous discharge should have blood tests done immediately. Instead, it was put off until the next day. Regardless, its reach had gone far beyond that of just those monitoring the anomaly that day. Within two days of the event, thousands reported headaches and fainting. Within three days, millions. After a day or so of those symptoms, victims suffered deadly hemorrhaging, followed by large emissions of yellow gas postmortem.

In the new world, gas masks are worn indoors, and only those with full airtight suits dare trek outside. Every time we eat or drink, we take our masks off and do so as quickly as possible, knowing any breath could be the one that inhales the yellow spores. Not everyone died in the event. Just enough to collapse governments, and the rest of the killing we mostly did ourselves. What remains is not human. We no longer live out the function of humans. Life on earth now is primal, animal. Because Dr. Robert Gordon needed to know what lurks in the nothing.

The Maw

I could hear the sound of grinding and crunching so loud in my head. Vibrating and echoing in my skull as the noise outside my own cranium trickled in with a faint attempt at overcoming the thunderous violence roaring between my ears. It was all in vain, as all I could comprehend was shades of black covering my peripherals while spewing gore soaked my eyelids. But I did not see through my eyes, more so behind them, like I could turn my head side to side at the neck and peer within a prison of bone and nerves spiraling out of control. All black inside, but for the two open portals allowing the light outside this hell to sweep in and glare along the landscape like the beam of a lighthouse searching across blackened night waters swirling into fathomless depths. I could tell that my body was moving, that I was still there. What I could not do, however, was control it, or even understand it. It was still just a surge of energy guiding my motions and actions, something that I could barely comprehend. The blood and torn flesh that had splattered into my face blocked my view, stopping me from putting together any clues that might help me to discover what was going on. It was when the sounds around me began to ring louder, as the cracking of bones between my jaw had ceased, that the images also became clearer.

I recognized this place. I stood in between the row of theater seats, going up a step with each row. Above me was a balcony with additional tiered seating. I was in the center of the stairs on the main floor facing the exit up the stairs, breathing deeply, posture tall and wide like that of an animal performing an intimidation display. The theater was not large. It had only eight rows of seats, and five red-fabric seats on either side of the stairs. I could hear shrieks that I would have guessed were inhuman had it not been for my complete knowledge that some terrible violence had occurred to many people here just moments ago.

I peered around me to see four or five bodies, the actual count difficult to number as they had been so horrifically injured and dismembered.

A whimper came from behind me. It was soft, then squeaking, then followed by sniffles and sobs. I turned to see a naked woman alone on the small stage. The lights above hit my eyes, bubbling and flaring. Then the stage itself began to flow like the red curtains that hung down onto it. The woman was sitting still, I was sure of it, but then she wobbled and rippled like water running down a rapid. As her body vibrated before me, she began to change. Not much. Small bits and pieces, but I could see a shift. She was crying, the sort of ugly heinous crying someone does at a dearest love's funeral. Her face was buried in her hands as she screamed and sobbed, lifting it for only a moment to peer out. Just a moment. A fraction of a second. Even through the strobing bubbly lights popping up everywhere around me, the sounds of screams echoing through my whole body, and the flow of the stage and the rippling of the girl, I saw it.

The girl—she was my Alexis. What was she doing here? Why was she on the stage? What was this place? Then it all came flooding back into my head, bringing with it an instant torrential current of rage coursing through my veins.

This place, the Peep Show, they called it. Girls dancing on this stage while disgusting old men sat fat in their chairs watching with devious eyes, scanning the bodies of these young women with perversion. One moment, I was in a chair. My friends and I were here on vacation. I insisted that I didn't wish to attend this, but my friends were just as persistent in their desire for me to come along. It was just as vile as I'd predicted when the show started. But I thought I would sit through it and then leave as soon as possible. Until I saw it. Everything around me grew vibrant, and sounds began to fuse together, just before I recognized the girl on stage. The previous girl was a blonde, but this one was a brunette. She had been dancing for almost three minutes already, and I had only just noticed it. She was my fiancée. My Alexis. What she was doing onstage, or why she was even in Amsterdam, was beyond me entirely. But all at once, my body was overcome with an insatiable bloodlust. These men, all of them in this theater staring at her, looking at her nude skin with foul fantasies floating in their minds. Whistling and moaning while others begged her to commit other vile acts onstage. Then I was gone.

My body remained to enact a terrible vengeance upon the perverted onlookers of my beloved Alexis, but my mind hid inside while some other entity entirely directed my rage. With a flash of crimson-soaked memories, I saw what I had done. After I'd lost control, like some sort of a beast, I lunged at the nearest onlooker and bit into his neck, peeling meat off between my teeth. Heavy blows to the head followed over and over, collapsing the skull in on itself. I then proceeded to leap onto a horrified attendee who, in his terror, had still yet to stand up to run. Person by person, transgressor by transgressor, I grabbed all that I could and ripped into them with my teeth and hands alike. Snapping at smaller bones while twisting and tearing limbs off at the joints. My teeth fracturing in my jaw as I chewed and crunched through bone. It had all come back to me, but now the rest of the grotesque perpetrators that had gazed on my beloved and stolen her innocence would pay with a brutal punishment.

As the memory of what had provoked my rage came forth, so too did the animalistic savagery that had just moments ago possessed me. Snarling, I ran out the front of the theater and was met by two security guards. I pounced on one of them, and, in an attempt to stop his face from being struck, the man stretched out his arms to intercept me. As my weight pummeled the security guard to the ground, I clamped down on the hand of his outstretched arm. Violently shaking my head back and forth, I managed to loosen the bone and flesh enough to tear clean a bite from him. Simultaneously, my hands found his throat and squeezed tightly till his windpipe collapsed.

The second guard kicked my head hard, dazing me as I fell off the man on his back, who was now gagging and gurgling on his own blood. From behind my eyes, I watched as my body arose and I snarled at the lone guard. Sprinting forward in a blitzing charge, I evaded the overhead haymaker blow the man was attempting and tackled him at the waist. Holding his arms down with my own, I gnawed and chewed on his face, devouring any chunks of flesh I managed to tear loose. When the man stopped struggling and screaming, I quickly leaped off of him toward the exit doors.

Out into the neon-lit night I roared. The city streets were crowded with people, some screaming in terror, more laughing and strutting without a care in the world. But as those around me who had not been witness to the massacre in the theater began to notice the abundance of gore decorating my mouth and clothes, they too screamed and ran. I screamed back with a potent fury, bearing my teeth, which dripped guts and tendons. The night was cool, and no clouds were out to obscure the stars' shine. The road was narrow, and it quickly became a canal of dark water. On the other side of the canal was another road with more shops and stores, where onlookers shouted in horror as the screams began to infect more and more bystanders.

Then as the commotion raged on, the sounds all drifting into my head as one indistinguishable entity, the lights dancing across the water in a display of flexibility and elegance, I seemed to have lost the purpose of my hatred, which had just a moment ago boiled so excruciatingly hot. Hunched over slightly, with my eyes pinned upward, watching the terrified tourists and locals flee in horror, I panted deep breaths. The noise of the sirens assaulted my ears and echoed deeply just as a vehicle careened around the corner, then violently jolted as it stopped right in the middle of the road I stood on. On the roof of the vehicle, lights began flashing and beaming, swirling before me, as if to tell me something. As if to remind me. Then within the hypnotizing luminous churn of color, I saw it. I had seen images in the rays of blazing brilliance. I saw my Alexis. On a stage, she stood alone. Dancing, performing. Showing herself to droves of crude, lustful men. A heat seared into my neck as I felt every muscle in my body tense with unfathomable ferocity.

As I snapped back from my delirium, a man stood alone in the streets before me. He must have been watching too. He must have violated her perfection with his loathsome eyes and abhorrent thoughts. I growled and hollered as this sole victim approached, before violently dashing toward him. He reached up, holding something, and began shouting at me in words I could not understand. As the world around me continued to twist and distort, I couldn't quite make out what he was holding either. But soon he too would pay for what was done to my beloved Alexis.

THE KNOCKING

"Are you gonna get that?"

I tilted my head curiously toward Danny. "Get what?" I then looked back toward the TV screen and continued playing our game unfazed.

"The door?" Danny responded, seeming slightly irritated, or maybe confused.

I was very invested in the game we had been playing the past few hours, so I wasn't exactly bothering to understand what Danny was getting at, but I didn't want to be rude.

"What about the door, dude?" I asked.

Danny sat up in his seat and asked, "You don't hear that?"

"Um ... ," I started. "No, I don't hear anything." At this point, I figured Danny was trying to be funny. Doing a poor job of it, but trying.

I instantly focused back on the game, but then Danny stood up sharply, admittedly jolting me a bit. "Dude, what are you doing?" I asked as I paused our game.

"Bro you don't hear that?" Danny said while moving his eyes from the door back to me, then back to the door again.

"No, I don't hear anything. What are you hearing?" At this point, I was starting to get anxious, more by just how Danny was acting than the supposed noise.

"That knocking? You don't hear the knocking on the door?" Danny was backing up to the wall as he asked me, clearly distressed.

I listened but could hear nothing. It was nine o'clock when Danny had arrived at my house, and we had been playing games for hours. At this point, it was one in the morning, and everyone in my house was asleep. With the game paused, it was, well, completely silent.

"No, I don't hear any knocking. But you're wigging me out, man. Relax." I said in a sort of teasing tone in an attempt to lighten the mood.

"Dude, it's right there!" Danny exclaimed, pointing at the door and touching the far wall with his other hand, almost as though connecting with the wall somehow distanced him farther from the door. He was panicking, breathing fast and hard.

"Bro, relax. What's the matter?" I got up out of my chair and looked at the door. "I'll go check, dude. Don't sweat it."

I began for the door when I felt a hand jerk me back by the wrist.

"No!" Danny screamed as he pulled at my arm, tugging it back, desperately trying to restrain me.

I turned, startled, to face him and pulled my arm back. I started to respond to him, but before I could get a word in, Danny yelled out again.

"Don't open it, don't open it!" Now with tears in his eyes and his back to the wall farthest from my bedroom door. He began to sink to the floor and curled up in a fetal position.

I stood over him completely lost as to what was going on, but also felt the tingle of fear running down my spine purely from how hysterical Danny was acting. "What's going on? Are you alright?" I asked as I leaned down to check on him.

Through his sobbing, he began to mumble, "It's talking … it's talking to me. Don't you hear it?"

My skin turned to ice. I was petrified. No clue as to what Danny was talking about, but just hearing what he had said and the way he suddenly became erratic was enough to freak me out. "Who? Who is talking to you?"

Sniffling and cowering, Danny looked up at me. "The man at the door. He's yelling at me."

As if I was not already shaken up enough, I felt my legs tremble and my stomach drop. I slowly turned toward my bedroom door and listened.

Nothing. I heard nothing. All I could hear was Danny crying on the floor. "Dude, I don't hear anything. Are you sure?" My voice shook as I struggled to get the words out. The thought of a man at my door at 1:00 a.m. was horrifying, and though I could hear nothing, Danny's behavior was enough to make me worried.

"He," Danny started before choking up. "He ... he ..." Danny continued to fumble on for some time.

"Hey, bro, it's okay. It's gonna be okay," I told him as I knelt down and put my hand on his shoulder. At this point, I knew I needed to buck up and attempt to be a voice of reason, even if I was terrified. But just as I thought I was getting a grip on myself, Danny was able to finish what he had been fumbling over.

"He wants me to let him in so he can kill me."

Danny buried his face in his arms and sobbed after his statement. I started to tear up a little and looked at the door. Could he be serious? Could there be someone at the door? If so, why couldn't I hear anything? No. No one was at my door, I started to convince myself in my head. No one could possibly be at the door. I began to breathe normally again and straightened up.

"Danny, no one is at the door. Calm down," I said confidently. I knew it was my duty as his friend to snap him out of it. I wasn't sure what was making him suddenly act like this, but I knew feeding into it was not the right answer.

"There is! There is!" Danny shouted back, with his face buried in his palms as muffled sobs seeped through.

"Dude, quiet down!" I whispered in my head but I yelled at Danny, "You are gonna wake my parents up!" At this point, I was getting over it. He had me all worked up, and now he was going to get me in trouble too.

"He's at the door. You have to hear it, he's right outside the door. He's banging on the door!" Danny said while still crying.

I knew what I had to do. The only way to stop this was to break his illusion. If the door was open, he couldn't claim that someone was at the door anymore. Problem solved. I was 99 percent sure he was not pretending or trying to play a prank, because his reactions were very genuine and his tears were very real. So he must just be imagining things. I had to show him it was just in his head. I started for the door when I heard a shriek from behind me.

"NO!" Danny cried as he leaped on me. "You can't, you can't!" he repeated as he pulled me back.

"Dude, get off of me!" I shouted as I shook him loose. He then dropped to the floor and grabbed hold of my leg, begging me not to open the door.

"Please, Eddie, please! Don't open it, just don't open it! He's going to kill me, he wants to kill me!"

His cries were foul to hear, and sounded like someone who was wounded. His fear was almost contagious. His horror was so profound I was sure he had to have lost his mind. I had to convince him to open the door for himself. That was the only way.

"Danny, you are hearing things, I promise you. Why would I want you to open the door if anyone was going to hurt you?"

"I don't know," Danny replied, whimpering.

"I wouldn't," I continued "And why would I hear nothing if someone was yelling and banging on the door?"

"I don't know," Danny repeated.

"You are hearing things. I don't know why, but you are hearing things. Open the door for yourself so you can see you are okay. Then we can just go to sleep, all right, man?" I tried to sound as rational and as calm as possible. I had never been through anything like tonight, or ever had to talk to someone like this before, so I was just doing my best to reason with him.

"Don't make me." Danny pleaded with tears streaming down his face.

"I'm not making you do anything." I had to convince him it was the best thing to do for his own sake. "I'm just telling you this is all in your head, and the only way to prove that to yourself is to open the door. I'm right behind you."

Danny stood up. I felt my stomach drop again. I wasn't sure he would do it, and now I wasn't sure I actually wanted him to do it. But he couldn't know that. We slowly moved toward the door, the sound of Danny's sniffling and our footsteps the only thing audible in the room. Danny slowly reached for the door handle.

"You really don't hear it?" Danny asked one last time as his hand closed around the doorknob.

"No. I can't hear anything."

I could hear the whine of the doorknob slowly turning, and my heart began thumping harder and harder with every beat. The door had barely begun to crack, revealing the darkness of the hallway outside my room. Then suddenly the door lashed open violently. For a second, I thought it was Danny who had ripped the door open, but I quickly realized I was horribly wrong.

Danny squealed as he was snatched up into the air. I fell backward to the floor and screamed out in horror. Danny was suspended in the air, but nothing was holding him. I could hear the sound of ripping flesh and screams coming from Danny while blood spewed onto the carpet. I cowered, balling myself up screaming on the floor, too terrified to do anything to protect myself, or my friend. I could hear Danny gargling on his own blood and the sound of bones snapping as his body began to contort. His cries of pain continued, only interrupted by him begging it to stop.

"Ple …" Then the sound of blood pouring from his mouth. "Please stop."

I covered my ears. I could not bear to hear his agony. But his howling was too loud. I couldn't drown it out. I laid there, hearing the most horrific sounds I never knew even existed. Then suddenly, it stopped.

I slowly lifted my head up from the cover of my arms to see my friend, eviscerated, on the floor. Snapped, broken, disemboweled, his blood covering the walls and ceiling. I could not comprehend what I was seeing. I screamed as the door suddenly whooshed shut. But nothing was there to shut it.

Then I heard it. Something began knocking on the door. Over. And over. And over. I shriveled into a ball again. I heard it. Now I could hear it all. I did not know I could reach a level of terror anything further than where I was when I heard a quiet hoarse voice call out to me.

"Let me in. Let me in."

I heard my parents' bedroom door open and my father's heavy footsteps followed by his burly voice.

"What the hell is going on in there? Do you know what time it is?"

I leaped to my feet and threw my body against the door. I could feel my dad's weight on the other side of the door as he attempted to open it.

"No, Dad, no, don't open it! Don't open the door!" I screamed. My hands were shaking as I reached out to lock the door to prevent anyone from opening it and letting it get to me.

"Edward, open the door. Now, son, open the door!" My dad was jiggling the doorknob when I heard him say. "Is this blood? What's happening, is everyone all right?"

I quickly pulled at my dresser and then pushed it up against my door, knowing my dad's next move would be to kick the door down. I couldn't let it get to me. All that time, even as my dad was trying to open the door, the knocking never stopped, and the voice had only grown louder.

"Let me in. Let me in."

I had gotten the dresser firmly shoved against the door, and my dad luckily could not get the door to budge. When for a moment, the knocking stopped. I listened in closer. I leaned in, hoping that maybe it had left. My whole body shuddered when I heard the voice roar out, "Let me in so I can kill you." Then the knocking became a bashing, as if the entity were trying to break down the door to satisfy its need to get to me. To kill me.

I just want you all to know this is not your fault. I hear the sirens now, and I know they are going to break the door down. Mom and Dad, I just want you guys to know this is not your fault at all, and I love you both so much. I know you can't hear it. I know you called the police 'cause you didn't know what else to do. I just wanted everyone to know what happened to us. It's still knocking. It's still telling me what it wants to do to me. Goodbye.

—Eddie

WATCHER IN THE BLACK

Behind conspiring stars, awaits a watcher in the black.
His power brought forth through evocation,
That feeble minds will find abstract.

A silent realm he inhabits,
Yet he hears the cosmos stories. A reality of endless void,
But still your world he sees.

He walks on suns,
Through black holes he ascends. I am his envoy,
And he is the end.

Doran's Prayer

I knew the Culler before he became a form of hatred and anger. I knew the Culler before he unleashed the bloodshed we had set out to relinquish. I knew the Culler when he was merely Doran.

Doran and I had grown up in a small town called Weindale. In our formative years, it was known to be a trading hotspot as it lay between two major cities. Travelers who passed by often found Weindale the perfect place to rest and barter on the midway of their journey. I still remember the town vividly. The busy streets crowded with all different walks of life. The shops and homes made of clay and brick. I still walk those streets in my head sometimes. I see all the familiar faces of my past. Carpenters, potters, and blacksmiths sweating as they work for their day wages. The other children in town laughing as they played war in the streets. Doran and I never played those games, though. Our parents forbade violence. Even if it was pretend. The church told us through the Word of God that violence meant damnation. No, neither Doran nor I would play war. War found our town, though. War took our town.

That was many years ago now. Almost like a different lifetime. Weindale was burned to the ground. My parents were slaughtered. Luckily, I did not witness that myself, and at such a young age, the image may have defiled me. Doran was not so lucky. We were both there when his parents were butchered in the church. We were all hiding on holy ground in hopes our God would save us. God failed to parry the blades that cleaved Doran's parents to pieces. I still wonder, in my most private moments, if we were spared that day for a purpose, Doran and I. By blind luck, or perhaps fate, we both escaped through the back of the church while the rest of the townsfolk taking refuge there were slaughtered. Against all odds that we should have been caught and had our throats slit, we somehow escaped Weindale entirely. Running across the hillsides, looking back only when we were sure no one was following us. Another image was seared into my memory. A memory that was triggered now by the sound of echoing screams, or the sight of distant smoke. Weindale engulfed in fire. The sound of the flames crackling competing with the screams of my family and friends to fill my sickened ears. In that moment, everything changed. Not just for the obvious reason of our home being annihilated. I dropped to my knees on that warm hillside in spring and clutched my hands together to pray to my God. Doran followed suit. I prayed for guidance in these darkest hours. I prayed for protection from the murderous warriors who raided our home. I prayed that Doran and I may find peace once more. I thought Doran's prayers would be much in line with my own. I was wrong.

I did not know of Doran's prayer until many years passed. After the destruction of Weindale, we fled to Roseden, a town just east of where my cousin lived. Life went back to a simple routine for a while, but never back to normal. I devoted myself to the teachings of the church. I followed the customs before, as my parents had taught. Now, though, I would become devout. I sought to use God's peace to rectify the horrors that had befallen the countryside. Doran, however, had changed in a far more drastic and violent means. The very first day we had arrived in Roseden, Doran made an oath, being sure that I bear witness to it.

"Know this, Casten. I will see them all to hell, where the lake of fire will drown their flesh for all eternity. I will not part ways with this earth, nor shall I flee to the comforts of heaven until those who committed these terrible atrocities are on the leash of Baphomet."

Through my readings, I knew that God was appalled by violence of any means, but the crusades did tell us that holy wars may be waged to save the followers of God. So I did not try to persuade him against his newfound oath. Instead, we would train in our polar-opposite arts, often side by side. I sat and read scripture while Doran practiced his sword stroke. I studied profound passages as Doran trained his body to become stronger. Our goals were the same, our methods contradictory.

Many nights Doran would awaken screaming. I presumed nightmares of his parents' murder haunted him, and upon many inquiries, Doran confirmed them as such. Now looking back, I fear Doran told me those lies to keep my mind at ease. It was those nights, as well as each passing day without his family, that fueled Doran's rage. He would train harder each day, as if the pagan invaders would strike Roseden at any moment. Until finally, the moment Doran had been training years for came. Roseden was besieged by the pagans.

I'd almost forgotten what these savages looked like. My memories of Weindale's demise mostly lingered on the flames, and the screams. But upon seeing the first of them shrieking a horrible war cry as he plunged his axe into a fleeing woman, it all came back to me. I stood in front of the church in horror watching the nightmare of my childhood play out in a new town. More children would end up like Doran, I thought. Broken. Angry. Vengeful. More than a dozen of them wielding swords and shields, axes and bows, spears and daggers. The town guard stood no chance, slain by the raiders in quick decisive fashion. I awaited my death with acceptance. I would not fight. My life's work to that point told me "Thou shalt not raise sword against shield, and we shall not learn war anymore." Doran, contrarily, had not learned these lessons. The church doors creaked open behind me, and out from the holy halls Doran met me at my side.

"I will see them all to hell." Doran said, drawing his broadsword.

My friend looked at me one last time. He appeared almost sad. A single tear betrayed him, sliding down his face to reveal his pain. At the time, I thought his sorrow was for a goodbye. We had been by each other's side as long as I could remember, and this was farewell. Now I know his mourning was not for the impending departure from our friendship. Unbeknownst to me in that moment, Doran knew this would be the last time I would look upon him as himself, as a man. After this day, Doran would become something else entirely.

Doran, wearing his iron cuirass and bearing his sword, boldly took toward the band of brutes. Some of the pagans appeared confused, maybe even offended, that a lone swordsman would walk upon them. The one I had seen slay that helpless woman just moments before, wore red paint striped down his face and animal pelts covering where his leather armor failed him. He roared a blasphemous call as he raised his axe, still dripping peasant blood, before charging to end Doran. In a display of his years of preparation and rage, Doran effortlessly gripped his hilt at both ends, providing more leverage for his upward stroke. The blade ripped up through the air and the pagan's skull alike, just as easily through one as the other. The remaining barbarians screeched at the sight of their fallen, and all at once, they advanced on Doran with frightening fury.

Doran's training again showed itself fruitful as he parried one blade, then the next from two different attackers, following the momentum of his defensive sword strokes to drive his blade forward and run through a third assailant. My astonished awe was shattered into a sickening sorrow. Too many. Doran's impressive feats ended just as quickly as they began. By the time Doran had killed just two of the men, the rest of the horde surrounded him and hacked through the back of his head. My grief forced out tears and cries of pain. My best friend, my brother, had made a vow. I knew he would never forgive himself in the next life, and his agony would be mine. Truly no one has ever mattered to me as much as Doran, and now I had witnessed him be slain.

The monstrous men turned their scowls toward me, their next victim. The first had war cries spewing from his mouth. Another screamed out in victory after slaying the swordsman, and the next coughed out six inches of steel, the blade covered in brains and teeth. Behind the man stood Doran. His sword had pierced through the back of the barbarian's skull and came out through his mouth. Doran's eyes seared with hellish hatred, dripping in a mixture of barbarian blood and his own.

"How?" I murmured.

I had just witnessed Doran's skull caved in with an axe. I knew it; with my own eyes I'd confirmed it. How did he stand up? Much less still have the strength to wield a blade? Perhaps it was blind luck that nothing vital was struck, perhaps a miracle of our God, but either way would suffice for me.

Doran retracted his blade from the mouth of the madman and slashed at the head of the nearest attacker, then punctured the chest of the next. Swift strikes, one attack leading to another, Doran strung together four killing strokes. Again, though, their numbers proved too great for one man. A spear thrust drove through Doran's neck, the spearhead cracking through the bone. My friend dropped to his knees, dead once more. The pagans did not leave anything to chance this time, however, the remaining lot cleaving down on Doran's torso, ensuring his demise.

I dropped down to my knees and clasped my hands together for one last time. I closed my eyes not to avoid the sight of my death—I did not fear that—but instead to see more clearly the visage of my God as I prayed to him this final time before joining him in his kingdom. The stomping of incoming murderous steps did not falter my prayer, but the sudden sound of colliding metal once more and the screams of agony in pagan tongues did. As I opened my eyes, while still on my knees with my hands positioned to speak to our Lord, I saw Doran there again unleashing his wrath upon the wicked. Now sure that Doran was some sort of monster, the pagans no longer fought him. They would flee in terror in hopes to avoid his steel, but they would instead just receive it in the back. Doran cared not that the men had surrendered. They would all face his judgment until only one remained. It seemed as though not only was Doran incapable of death, but his body would not fatigue, as though an inextinguishable fire fueled him from within. The last of the pagans begged with words that neither Doran nor I could understand, but clearly, through his sobs and cowering, the man was begging for his life. Doran grabbed at the man's throat with barbaric strength, raising the cowering raider from his knees to meet his own gaze.

"You'd be better off begging to the devil," Doran snarled, drawing his dagger. "As a matter of fact, you can beg him when you get there."

Doran drove the blade into his victim's abdomen, then ripped upward into the heart.

The brutality of Doran's killings showed me that he was not purely fighting for God's will but also for his own malice. Deep down, I'd known that from the beginning, but this display of barbarism made this fact undeniable. To that end, Doran's vengeance was not nearly complete. Many, many more would be slain by my friend.

Soon tales of Doran's feats would spread across the land. A man who could be slain, only to rise by the will of God, to smite the nonbelievers for their blasphemies. Those who had stood at the edge of battle and witnessed Doran run through by blades, only to stand against his enemies once more to return the favor, would spread his tale with righteous favor.

"He is protected by the archangels!" they would cry.

"The archangel Michael incarnate is upon us, to punish the sinful pagans." The peasants would claim.

Doran's legend would be that of a warrior from the mouth of heaven and the army of God, inflicting the will of the divine. That would be Doran's legend for all those who had not seen what he had truly become. I did not watch Doran's killings from afar, or hear tales of his glory fall upon my ignorant ears. I stood by his side; I followed Doran into battle. Not to assist in his murderous rampage, but to pray for the soul of my friend. I witnessed his brutality firsthand and saw the changes in his form that no others would speak of. Time after time, Doran would meet a momentary end by the hand of his enemies, only to resurrect and impose his judgment upon his would-be killer. But his return to life was never without cost. His wounds would heal, but never naturally. His skin would bear the scars of his attacks, and his bones would form back in unnatural ways. Doran had become a grotesque image of flesh and twisted bone, covered in copious scars. His face was no longer that of my friend's; instead, teeth lay upon his cheeks and jaw. Swirling scar tissue compromised his face. Flesh would often heal back over his eyes as well as his mouth after being struck in the head, making him rip away at the skin to allow sight and breathing once more. Doran was a monster, and as time passed, more people saw the form he had taken. The tales of angels and godly intervention slowly faded, giving rise to a new name. No longer Doran, the masses would know him as the Culler. One who was sent here for the task of removing the pagans, but this time with a less appealing connotation.

The pagan war camps began moving on, finding their reasoning and understanding that the Culler could not be stopped. Staying in these lands raiding towns and villages was not worth their lives. Only a few proud warriors remained. One of whom not only refused to retreat but chose to seek out the Culler. This pagan was a vicious war chief. One who went by the name of Romak.

Romak had led raids on many towns and slain more warriors than most men would ever look upon. His violent urges would get the better of him and often cause him to dismember his dead opponents. No man had ever faced Romak and his hordes and lived to tell about it. The only accounts of his cruelties came from peasants who had witnessed these atrocities and fled to neighboring villages. Romak, much like the Culler, was a horror story. One meant to be told to the enemy to drive them mad with fear before the battle had even begun, and now Romak himself sought to take the Culler's head.

It was well known to all that the Culler stayed in Roseden. Doran liked it that way. He wanted all the savages to know where he laid his head at night. Up to that point, it had kept every last one of the pagans far away from Roseden's gates. This was a warning that Romak took as an invitation.

Doran had heard the rumors that a lone warrior was coming for him and, of course, did not believe it. Ever since dawning the title of the Culler, dozens of men would flee at the sight of his monstrous form. All men knew the Culler couldn't be stopped. All men knew the Culler was death. But to Doran's disbelief, one morning, as the sun rose and teased the night sky with its orange gleam, a lone pagan approached Roseden. The warrior screamed out for the Culler to face him, with a broken accent that told me he had barely learned to speak our language. Nonetheless, it implied to Doran that this savage wanted to learn to communicate with him. That alone grabbed Doran's attention.

Doran donned his armor, sheathed his sword, put on his greaves, and set out to stain another morning with blood.

"Will this ever end?" I pleaded with him as he passed through the doors of the church where we resided. "Doran? Please. You can't do this forever. Look what it's done to you."

Doran looked back at me with his mangled figure, one eye nearly shrouded by tattered skin, the other lower and deeper in the skull than ever naturally intended.

"Casten, you are the only reason I've not gone entirely mad. You still pray for me, you still hold hope for me. I will forever be grateful." Doran said this with his sunken eye showing his tears for the first time since he had walked out those same church doors to slay the Culler's first victims. His tears showed me that somewhere behind that mass of carnage and hatred, he still sat mourning his family. Consumed by his need for vengeance, that little boy who watched his mother and father be slain still sat behind the Culler's eyes calling out in agony. Agony that he could only momentarily cease by inflicting his pain on others.

Doran walked away toward the town's gate to meet his foe. As I had always done, I followed him on that cold fall morning. The half-lit skies looked down upon the two warriors with glee. The most fearsome fighter of God, the most ferocious pagan blasphemer. They stood in front of Roseden alone. There were no two greater warriors to have ever stood across from each other.

"Pagan." The Culler called out to his enemy.

The two stood roughly thirty feet apart. Romak was adorned with human spines and femurs, sights that would frighten lesser opponents. He wielded a great axe with a dull iron blade, chips and splinters showing the blade's age and experience. The bearded barbarian called back to the Culler.

"You are not immortal," Romak snarled and beat the handle of his great axe upon his chest. "I will drink from your skull!"

Romak meant his threat, as he immediately charged in a horrifying display of fearlessness. Doran raised his broadsword and prepared for a counterstrike. The fool, Doran must have thought. To wildly charge with a cumbersome weapon. This would be over quickly.

Romak cleaved overhead, and Doran raised his sword to glance off the blade and use the momentum to carry through a strike of his own. Then Doran's blade found itself meeting no resistance. What was this? Suddenly Romak shifted his feet to a wider stance, distributing his weight so he may easily shuffle to one side. Caught off guard, Doran quickly attempted to bring his blade into a vertical defense to stop the misdirected attack incoming from the axe's blade. Again, no resistance, but before Doran could realize the axe head never struck, the hilt end of the axe's handle smashed into Doran's face, shattering the fused bone. Before Doran could recover from the concussive strike, Romak pulled his blade back once more and cleaved into Doran's abdomen. In one motion, Romak dislodged his blade from Doran's ribs and swept his feet out from underneath him with the axe's long wooden grip. Romak looked down on Doran's bloodied corpse and raised his weapon above his head, roaring in victory.

Doran sat up and looked around for his sword. He had dropped it somewhere when his face had been struck. Romak looked down at Doran, confused and bewildered. The moment of astonishment allowed Doran to find his blade and rise to his feet once more.

"What magic? How do you do this?" Romak questioned, still holding his axe, ready for the next attack.

"Come forth, and I will show you the place from which I draw my power." Doran remarked with his gruesome stare locked on Romak.

Romak yelled another war cry and charged as he had done before, this time cleaving wildly to behead Doran. The strike missed its mark, as Doran ducked beneath the powerful swing and then attempted to counter with a stabbing thrust with his sword. Romak quickly swung his rear foot back to shift his weight, allowing his lower hand to rise up and smash Doran's blade away with the hilt of his axe. With one more shift of his feet, Romak was again in position to quickly strike down with his axe, gashing Doran's already-mangled face. The weight of Doran's dead body pulled down on Romak's axe, which was still stuck in Doran's skull. Slamming his foot against the side of Doran's head, Romak peeled the blade out from Doran's face. As Doran lay dormant, Romak smashed down with his axe numerous times, creating a pile of gore that was unrecognizable.

"No. What is this? How?" Romak said, stepping back from the rising body of torn flesh. "You will die!" Romak demanded as he assaulted the bloody corpse once more.

Slashing and hacking, kicking and stabbing, Romak would cleave at the pile of meat until he was sure the bones were no more than dust.

"Here is your immortal," Romak declared to Roseden, holding one hand open, gesturing toward the pile of Doran's gore. "The Culler has been culled."

Romak stood screaming at Roseden, both hands now gripping his axe, which he held overhead in a display of triumph. His cheers of victory were interrupted by the slimy sound of contorting flesh. Romak turned to see the carcass rising slowly, bits of blood and remains shifting in an attempt to create a human form. Romak shrieked in anger, stopping only when the deformed body raised its arm to grip a piece of its face, peeling back skin to reveal an eye. The eye was burning with the loathing of Lucifer, piercing into Romak.

"You think killing me would be a victory?" Doran began, his skin still reforming to cover his exposed muscles and tendons. "Any man who has slain another, regardless if their cause is noble, no matter if it was in an attempt to defend their homes and families, is damned." Doran's fingers twitched and spasmed as they began to realign. "Beyond the black," he continued, "there is a door. I've been there many times. Men like us are doomed to visit this place, but I am cursed to travel there over and over again."

Romak had thrown the weight of his great axe around to smash Doran to pieces, but he no longer had the strength, or the will, to fight. Instead, he would witness the horror taking place before him and hear Doran's harrowing message.

"When your people ravaged my home and family, I prayed for the power to end you all. But when you drop to your knees and pray to something you don't understand, all ears are listening. I was granted that power, but with a price I could not yet comprehend as a boy. I've been to hell. I've drowned in the lake of fire. I've seen Satan's design. You will too. But I, I am damned to repeat this. Every time a blade strikes me down or an arrow punctures my heart, I fall from this world. These fleeting moments of existence seem so short to you all, when I die and am reborn. But I can assure you, those short moments here are a lifetime in the agony of hell. So every time I'm slain, I awaken with the pain of having suffered lashings of fire and claws of demons. And it reminds me of where you will all be going. It reminds me why I started this in the first place. All the pain, all the suffering is worth it when I take my trips to that place beyond the black and see the faces of all those who I've sent there. I will be seeing you again."

Whether hearing that my friend had made a deal with Satan to torture the souls of the living or the sound of Romaks screams as Doran tore him apart was worse, I still do not know to this day.

UNSHACKLED

"Time heals all wounds" is perhaps the most misleading statement a person could heed. Not necessarily out of ill intention, but more so misconception. Most wounds do heal in time, but it is erroneous to assume that one is the catalyst of the other. Time is unbound, unshackled, untamable. Nothing escapes the constant linear track that is the passing of time. The presumption that the never-ending passage of time can be attributed to something as enigmatic as healing, would be no more far-fetched than to assume the mere passing of time could cause love, or hate. It is the occurrences of the moments within the time itself that causes love, hate, and healing. The flow of time is ever present, so it may be easy to see where most people could confuse time's relevance to any given situation. But it is not time itself that will heal a wound. Time itself may continue to travel forward, while you revisit the same pain every day. This was the terrible realization Nolan had.

An older man, having turned eighty-one the past month, Nolan had lived only half a life. At the hopeful age of thirty-one, he had been married to his beloved Elly for ten years. He still remembered the way people laughed and mocked, doubted and rejected his young marriage. He didn't care. Nolan would marry Elly at twenty-one despite those who opposed their union. Even though everyone degraded his love for Elly, Nolan would not hate them. Because he knew what no one else could. He knew that he needed Elly the way only true love would inspire. Of course Nolan understood the criticism. How many young fools fall in love fast and spiral into disgust after? How many people make life-altering choices on the whim of their first love? Nolan understood that. So he did not mind the criticism. He welcomed it, as it would be one more way he could prove to the world that he truly loved his Elly more than words could detail. But life is not a love story. Nor is it fair. You can't reason with it, or bargain with it. Life is a tyrant. It will oppress and command you, with no room for deliberation. As events pass in time, you may not ask to undo them or plea for an appeal. At the age of thirty-one, his Elly would die.

The diagnosis was even more unbearable still, as the doctor told Nolan something that would alter the course of history on earth forever.

"If we had caught this one year earlier, we could have saved her. I'm sorry."

Nolan looked to his Elly and wept, begging her not to go, as if the choice was hers to make. "It will be okay, my love," Elly said softly as her Nolan held tightly onto her. "I'll always be with you."

But that was not true. Elly would not always be with him. Six months after the diagnosis, Nolan sobbed on his knees at the bedside of a corpse. His Elly was no longer there as she promised. He could not feel her presence the way that some hopeless optimists would claim you could. The stories of a place afterward, a paradise that we must all wait for. Nolan did not believe that. Even if he did, he could not trust that. Nolan would see his Elly again, and he refused to leave that up to a chance as slim as God or heaven. Nolan would see his Elly again. He would feel her again. He would love her always.

For three years, Nolan researched his options. Spiritual means were dismissed within days. For a short time, Nolan even studied resurrection. Another dead end. A career as a physicist had left Nolan closed-minded to the supernatural. So instead, he began delving further into something that would seem even more unlikely. To manipulate time itself. Nolan thought about what the doctor had said to him years ago.

"If we had caught this one year earlier, we could have saved her. I'm sorry."

One year could have saved her. One year. If time would refuse to let Nolan have his Elly, then he would go to war with time itself. The realization of his mission would ignite an even more powerful passion inside Nolan. Now it wasn't just a hope and a dream. Now he had a plan. Now it was no longer in the hands of an omnipotent being, nor was he being restrained by the chains of time. Now, unshackled, seeing his Elly was in Nolan's hands alone.

Starting in as good a place as one is able when attempting to bend time to one's own will, Nolan at least had an understanding of the challenge ahead, having been an accomplished and brilliant physicist for the past nine years. Nolan would zealously research and work on his project day and night, liquidating every asset he possessed to put toward the path to his Elly. This motivated work ethic would continue for five long years, until Nolan's realization finally occurred. This was not a task a man could complete in a lifetime. So much progress in five years while still seemingly accomplishing nothing at all. His deep understanding of quantum physics surpassed any breathing human, but time itself seemed to be striking back. Not only would time refuse Nolan the right to see his Elly, it would continue to march him closer to death with each passing day. By the time Nolan had discovered its secrets, he would be long dead himself.

However, this did not entirely deter Nolan. His work continued for years still. Painfully exhausting himself and every relationship he had in his life. His family had all but disowned him; his friends all but abandoned him. He never showed them a care, or effort of any kind. His life, his existence, was his battle with time. Viewed now by the ones who loved him as a crazed lunatic, a madman, a failure. But Nolan persisted, and soon his work would be rewarded.

Ten years after Nolan's journey to reunite with his Elly began, he had a breakthrough of astonishing proportions. Nolan discovered that not only was traveling to a different time possible, it was achievable through a machine he had the means to create. Of course, where Nolan's theories began years ago was the requirement of traveling faster than the speed of light. The faster past that speed one traveled, the slower time would pass. Until, hopefully, a speed could be reached where time could be manipulated altogether. Space and time are linked, they are one entity. But now, Nolan had a hypothesis. He had drawn up blueprints for countless machines, written down formulas for endless equations, and finally, he found the respective two that may in theory allow him to warp time and space into the verge of a wormhole.

Building this machine took nearly a decade; multiple prototypes were made and scrapped as Nolan perfected his design. The equation was promising, and the machine had to be perfect. The machine had to be capable of not only warping space but also of doing it precisely enough to decide where you would go. Each sleepless night working on the machine saved Nolan from a sleepless night in agony taunted by the reality of his Elly's death. Each bead of sweat he lost put one more ounce of hope in him that he may see her again. Years would take his father, then his mother. Years would take his ability to work through those long nights. However, with each victory that time celebrated, Nolan grew ever more driven.

As Nolan grew to the age of eighty-one, time began to pronounce its victory a moment prematurely. Nolan had finished his machine decades prior, but finding something capable of fueling it cost him the years between the machine's completion and his eighty-first birthday. But finally, it was done. Nolan's machine was completed. One more step needed to be taken to ensure full functionality of the time warper. A device to send him back to his current location. A mobile device to send him back to the time warper. Without that, his trip through time would have to be completed with no test run. If he failed, he would be sent somewhere unintentional with no means of return, or altogether killed. This was a risk Nolan had no choice but to take. If he sacrificed any more years to the completion of another device, time would conquer his life before he could be reunited with his Elly. Nolan had one shot at seeing her again. One chance to be with his love. A familiar feeling took over the old man. A feeling in his heart he had not felt since he was twenty-one years old. The feeling of everything telling him he was wrong. The feeling of everything being stacked against him and knowing that, through love, he was right. Nolan felt absolutely positive that his machine would take him to his love despite the detrimental odds stacked against him. Just as he had once felt undoubtedly positive about marrying his Elly against everyone's wishes.

Nolan turned on his machine, set the dial, and entered with tears overwhelming him. Not of delight from his life's work. Not from selfish pride boasting about his accomplishments, being the first and only man to break the chains of time. He was overwhelmed by the realization that he was just moments away from looking upon the perfection that was his Elly. Nolan would finally save her. Nolan would finally be whole again.

Awaking to nausea and momentary confusion, Nolan quickly realized his predicament. It had worked. Struggling to get to his feet, he was curious about how the time warp would affect his own age. His hypothesis was that he would not magically become younger like most Hollywood depictions of time travel so romantically insist. He was correct. Once he was able to push himself to his feet, his knees struggling to hold his posture as the nausea was still ever present after his pilgrimage, he inspected the surrounding area. He had landed in the middle of the street just ten minutes from his home. An absolutely remarkable amount of accuracy.

Nolan wasn't entirely sure whether he would end up appearing in the middle of the ocean, or whether he would warp into a solid object and crush himself instantly. To his pleasure and admitted surprise, the machine was nearly pinpoint accurate, all things considered. The exact year, though, was the next concern. Did he make it in time to save his Elly from her diagnosis? He did. Nolan wasn't positive what year it was, but he was positive he had saved his Elly. He could feel that he had rescued her as surely as he could feel his unyielding love for her. Without knowing, he knew. Now a short walk down the street was the last thing keeping him and his Elly apart. Barring one final issue.

As Nolan approached their home, he did so cautiously. The final true obstacle that needed to be conquered before Elly was all his once more was he himself. Whether or not defeating time or his thirty-year-old past incarnation would be more difficult, he was still unsure. What he was sure of was that if he himself had been thirty and a man approached his Elly claiming to be her long-lost love out of time, he would have killed him. So to be her love, Nolan would have to remove his impostor from the equation first. Nolan slowly snuck around to the backyard of his suburban home. The sliding glass door would be unlocked, as it always was. On Nolan's short walk, based on the clues that presented themselves throughout the neighborhood, he deduced that it was roughly between 11:00 a.m. and 2:00 p.m. No children playing in the neighborhood, schools had not let out yet. Bright like a sunny spring afternoon. Nolan felt confident that no one would be home. Furthermore, no cars sat in his driveway. The sliding glass door was, indeed, unlocked. Nolan found his way in with ease. The brutality he felt simply grabbing the kitchen knife was overpowered entirely by his excitement to be with Elly again. He was not exactly enthralled with the concept of murdering himself, but he had no choice. He knew that his younger self would instinctively assault him at the sight of a stranger in his home. Have him taken away by the police. Keep him from his Elly. If time could not keep Nolan from his Elly, he himself certainly would not either.

Another mundane day at the office, Elly was exhausted more mentally than physically. The redundancy of Human Resources at the County Plaza was what made her days so tiring. Not the labor of it. The promise of a dinner out from her dear husband loomed over her like a pending debt. She knew how much it meant to Nolan, still taking her out on dates nearly a decade after they'd been married. He always did these things to remind her his love had not faded a shade. Tonight, though, she was too drained to even comprehend the task of going home and changing to drive back into town. Instead, Elly would pick up a pizza on the way home. Nolan would surely understand, as he always did. She did feel slightly guilty canceling her dinner date. She knew not every man continued to show his spouse the same affection after all these years. She felt lucky in that way, but tonight she would tell her Nolan that she just doesn't have the energy and would instead like to watch a movie with him on the couch while eating an entire large pizza. He would enjoy that idea, she thought.

Elly pulled into the driveway and parked next to Nolan's car. Hopefully, he wasn't already all dressed up for the canceled date, she thought. She carried the warm box of pepperoni pizza inside, anxious to enjoy its contents. The aroma from the box had been mocking her hunger since she had picked it up. "Honey, I have a confession to make." Elly teasingly announced as she came through the front door. She used her foot to kick the front door shut before continuing toward the kitchen to set down tonight's dinner. "I hope you aren't all dressed up, baby." Elly hoped this would be a passive-enough statement to get the point across.

"Elly," a familiar but strange voice called out to her from behind.

Elly turned to face the stairwell where she had heard her name. The sight confused and startled her. A face as familiar as the voice, and just as strange. Elly's body jolted back, and she gasped, as she couldn't find words to match her bewilderment.

"Elly, baby, it's me." Nolan stepped toward her, the tears streaming down his face and his smile telling the story of what this moment meant to him. His life's work, all for this exact moment. There she stood. Alive and breathing, right before his eyes. There was his perfect Elly.

"Wha … I … wha …" Syllables came from Elly's mouth with no full comprehensible thoughts. She couldn't quite piece together the sight her eyes were explaining to her yet. It was Nolan. She knew every inch of her husband's face. Every detail of his image. The man standing before her, she knew, was Nolan. But how?

"I know, my love, it's a lot. I can explain it all."

Nolan kept his approach slow, first, to allow Elly time to interpret what she was seeing, and secondly, because his frail aged bones wouldn't allow a much faster pace despite his excitement.

"Are you …" Elly was finally finding words that could be put together in a sentence. "Are you sick? What happened?"

"No, my love. I'm better than I've ever been." Nolan's voice slipped into a sob as he had to force the final portion of his sentence out before his crying made speaking incoherent. "I love you so much, Elly. I missed you so much. I never stopped thinking about you. I always knew I'd be with you again." Nolan cried out as he embraced his Elly for the first time. He held her tight, and she held him the same way, still unsure of what was happening. His words confused her still, and she felt sick to her stomach with fear. Not of Nolan but for whatever was happening to him.

"Baby, I think we need to get you to a hospital." Elly said, fighting through her tears.

"No, no. I'm fine. I'm fine. I just need to explain everything to you, my love."

They stayed there, embracing each other for a short while. Nolan was content just holding on to her. He could have stayed there forever. Elly, though, was still in shock, and in desperate need of the answers Nolan had promised.

"Okay, Nolan, please tell me what's goi—," Elly began as she stepped back from him, but the sight of blood on his shirt caused her to interrupt herself. "Why are you bleeding? Baby, what's happening? I'm so scared." Elly broke down in a frightened panic. Her Nolan, her husband, was dying. So she thought.

"I'm not bleeding, dear. I'm okay." Nolan's response puzzled her.

"Wh-what do you mean? Whose blood is it?"

"I was attacked. I had to defend myself. But I'm okay now, dear. Everything is okay."

These answers were only raising questions as opposed to giving Elly any reasoning to what was happening.

"Attacked by who? Where? Please, Nolan, I'm so scared. Please just tell me what's going on." Elly begged Nolan to explain the situation.

Nolan wanted to give Elly all the details, but he didn't want this moment to end. His reunion with his love. His return to his Elly. He needed this moment.

"Nolan, tell me what's happening!" Elly shouted, no longer able to bear the secrecy.

Nolan looked at his weeping Elly with indescribable awe. Just as, if not even more beautiful than he remembered. More than that, she was just as beautiful a person as he remembered too. She was upset, and brought to panic, because of her worry for him. She didn't care that he was aged and worn down. He was still her Nolan.

"Nolan." Elly's voice was muffled as she cried into Nolan's chest while she called out to him.

"I have to explain something to you. I'm not from here, my love."

Elly curiously glanced up to Nolan.

"What do you mean not from here?"

Elly was now on the verge of a mental collapse. Too many strange happenings and statements with no clear answers in sight.

"I'm from a different time. Nothing happened to me. I'm just older." Nolan said this with a certain confidence. He knew the information would be jarring and expected her to dismiss him at first.

You mean, the future? You're Nolan in the future?" Elly whimpered. She was surely shaken, but she didn't respond as negatively as Nolan expected.

"Exactly."

"How? Why?" Elly continued to cry as the conversation went on, perhaps from the overload of emotions to this point.

"How." Nolan looked down at Elly, his eyes fixed on hers. "I built a machine. I built something to warp me through time. The why. That's the easy part. To see you again, my love. To be with you again."

Elly sniffled and wiped her nose before responding. "So I died?"

"Yes. You died very young. I had to go fifty years without you. Every day was torture knowing you were being held away from me by death. Knowing I couldn't have you. But I beat time for you, my love.

I defeated time so I could hold you again. Nothing will ever keep you from me."

Elly's eyes began to search back and forth, as if she was contemplating something that had just come to her. Nolan was confused, as he was so sure the moment he explained to Elly how he built a time machine for the sake of their love that she would be overjoyed.

"Where's Nolan?" Elly asked plainly.

"I … I am Nolan."

"No. Where is my Nolan?"

The words pierced Nolan's ears like a rusted blade, jagged and tearing through him.

"Elly, baby, I am your Nolan. It's me." Nolan held Elly's hands as he pleaded with her.

"His car was out front. He's here, where is he?" Elly persisted. Now all her other questions were secondary. Now she needed to know only one thing. Where was her husband?

"I … well, he …" Nolan's breathing was telling the story he couldn't put into words. Elly ran past him toward the stairs. "Elly, wait!" Nolan cried out, chasing after her as quickly as his aged joints would allow.

Elly reached the top of the stairs and headed toward her bedroom. A panic was building in her, a sense of impending doom. She wasn't exactly sure why she felt this dread. But as she pushed open the bedroom door, her dread was justified.

Nolan. Her Nolan lay on the floor. Blood stained the carpet on the perimeter around his body. Gashes were leaking on his upper back and neck. The wounds were no mystery, as the kitchen knife slathered in gore left no room for interpretation. Nolan had been murdered. Elly collapsed to meet her Nolan on the floor, and as blood soaked the carpet around him, tears would drench the carpet around her.

"Elly," the once-familiar and once-comforting voice now ripped a chill up her spine. The hairs on her neck and arms stood on end. "Elly, I can explain what happened."

"You." Elly turned back to face her husband's killer. "You murdered my Nolan." She looked up at the old man in disgust and anguish. "You came here to save me, and you butchered my husband."

"He attacked me, Elly. He attacked me when he saw me." This was not just a lie Nolan was telling Elly, but one he had told himself. He could never think of himself as a killer. Surely, if he were to hurt anyone, it would be for a good reason. Surely, Nolan would never murder anyone. Surely, Nolan was a good man.

"You stabbed him in the back. You killed him." Elly's sobs were joined by shrieks of pain and anger as the realization of her loss took hold. Her Nolan was dead. She would go on the rest of her life without her husband.

"I had to, Elly. I had to." Nolan pleaded.

Elly wanted to feel her Nolan one more time. She reached out to his corpse but did not dare touch it. Though she knew he was already dead, the fear of touching his body and feeling its lifelessness drowned her. She turned back to the horrific old man she had met just a few minutes earlier. The anguish in her eyes was so familiar to Nolan.

"You didn't come here for me, Nolan." Elly now understood what truly happened. "You came here to save yourself. You couldn't bear the pain of losing your Elly. The misery was too much of a burden, so you came here. You came here to take my Nolan so you wouldn't have to be alone anymore. You came here to make me suffer the way you did all those years."

Nolan's heart convulsed when he heard these words come from the mouth of his Elly. He wanted to rebut these terrible claims, but his throat was swollen with tears. All he could do was listen to his judgment.

"You aren't my Nolan. He is." Elly peered back at the mangled body of her beloved husband. "Now I will spend my entire life alone. Just like you."

The horrors of that day tore apart the hopes of an old man whose love drove him to do what he thought necessary to save his wife. The horrors of that day tore the heart out of a woman who thought she was coming home to her loving husband. But those consequences would be inconsequential in the grand macrocosm. Nolan traveled to a place that was not his and killed a man who was not him. Murder, though horrific, is not sparse in this world. Instead, the worst of all the things that occurred that day was that Nolan's machine sat dormant. It sat with its schematics and fuel, its research and instructions. Nolan's machine waited to be found. A power unbound awaited discovery. A power that would not have been earned by its finder. This kind of power, when unearned, has built no discipline. Power without discipline is always corrupt. Corruption with the power to unshackle time. That was the true horror of that day.

THE ONI

A warrior walked through the wood,
In search of calmness and air.
But on his unbeaten path,
An oni sat there.

The oni wore large black horns,
His eyes glimmered yellow.
The warrior drew his katana,
The oni greeted, "Hello."

Its skin a dim red,
Its robes tattered and old.
Its claws razor sharp,
Its blood ran ice cold.

No words to share.
The warrior would not speak to the beast.
His greeting must be a ploy,
For on hearts onis' feast.

The oni sat on a stump,
Surrounded by swords,
He must devour victims' flesh,
Then their blades the monster hordes.

A courageous shout before a charge,
The warrior was surprised,
For when the oni stood off his stump,
He towered nine feet high.

Snarling with curved canines,
Long thin white hair,

And a blade of his own,
Which followed his glare.

The warrior sliced at the throat,
The strike was quickly parried.
The warrior continued his assault.
The attacks were all varied.

Stabs and cuts thrown about,
In an attempt to end the foul demon.
But the oni was no fool,
Clearly unto this point he'd been unbeaten.

With the blades of fallen samurai,
Scattered all about,
The warrior knew the oni's power,
He began to feel doubt.

The oni kicked the warrior down,
A devastating blow.
Then turned his back on the swordsman.
"You've lost, samurai. Now go."

But the warrior's rage was relentless
At the sight of this monster.
He would not let it live,
He would not let it wander.

With the oni's back turned,
The warrior lunged and drove his sword deep.
Then he decapitated the demon,
For its head he would keep.

The warrior's laugh echoed far,
His judgment was fulfilled.
The trees the only witness,
To the blood that had been spilled.

His laughter grew louder,
As his skin turned to crimson.
And cracking through his skull,
Black horns had arisen.

Corrupted by his malice,
He took on a monstrous form.
Metamorphosis upon him,
He was a warrior no more.

The oni looked around,
His foe's blade now joined the others.
Then upon a stump he sat,
To rest and to recover.

By the time he'd gained stamina,
He saw just down the path.
A samurai approached sword in hand.
The sight of his form invited wrath.

Cycles of death,
For hate will breed hate
Slaying a man you've deemed a beast
Will a monster make.

DIABOLIC

"When will Daddy be home?"

Daddy won't be home, Terra said to herself.

But not to Rachel. Terra didn't have the heart to tell her daughter. Not yet. Maybe not ever.

Of course, one day she would have to tell Rachel. Just not tonight. Tonight had been painful enough. The long shower Terra had taken, using the sound of raining water to mask her wretched weeping, had been enough pain for tonight.

"I'm not sure, baby." Terra mustered up a response, her throat tight from swallowing the sorrow of the true answer.

Rachel was only six. Not old enough to comprehend why a Father would leave. Not young enough to simply forget he had ever been there. Rachel would one day realize he was never coming back, and the memories of him would haunt her for a lifetime. These thoughts filled Terra's head. She would carry not only the anguish of the love she lost but also the burden of knowing what this would do to her child. Her innocent Rachel.

"Mommy, I wanna see Daddy." Rachel said, rubbing her eyes, followed by a wide-mouthed yawn.

"Me too, baby. Me too. But it's time for bed."

Terra led Rachel to her bedroom and tucked her in as she always did. The night-light on, the door cracked, and as usual, told Rachel that she would be just down the hall. Terra's frequent night terrors as a child made her a paranoid mother. She remembered how dismissive her own mother and father were of her tormentor—the man in the closet—and how many horrified nights she would spend paralyzed with fear as she watched him stare at her from the closet.

No matter how much Terra begged and pleaded, her parents would send her back to her room, always reminding her that the man in the closet was in her imagination. He wasn't real.

Terra swore to herself that her daughter would never go through that. Not a single night of the dread she was forced to face alone.

But Rachel never had nightmares. Never came to her parents' room in tears, fearful of a lurking evil. Rachel slept peacefully, with no closet-dwelling monsters to bother her. Nonetheless, Terra made sure to make Rachel feel as safe and comfortable as possible, always leaving both Rachel's, and her own bedroom door cracked open.

"Good night, baby. Mommy loves you so much."

Terra kissed Rachel on the head and quickly turned away to hide the tears beginning to swell her eyes.

"Good night, Mommy. I love you so much too." Rachel replied softly as she closed her eyes.

Being strong for Rachel is all that matters now, Terra told herself. Be strong for Rachel.

Terra's own bed felt desolate. The space her husband used to inhabit was now a void. Her home felt like a prison of memories. A place where each wall, each picture, each place of comfort now held the agony of what once was, and will never be again.

Terra's heart tightened in her chest, and her legs tingled to the point of near numbness. As she lay there in bed, she turned her head. And there, in the closet, she saw it. Eyes and a heinous smile—the man in her closet staring right at her, grinning widely. Her breathing became sporadic, and the tightness in her chest began to spread across her body like a plague.

But in a blink, the eyes were gone. Just like that, nothing in the darkness. Terra tried holding back sobs, to no avail. Her husband was gone, and now, for the first time in thirty years, she'd seen the man who watched from the closet. He was so vivid. Seemed so real that Terra had felt fear for her life, and just like that, he was gone again. Too much. Too much for one day. Her body was as tired as her eyes were from crying. She had to rest, and somehow, even after being in a state of pure terror, Terra was able to fall asleep.

"Mommy."

"Huh?" Terra murmured as she lifted her head from the pillow, barely awake.

"Mommy, get up." Rachel was standing in the doorframe of Terra's bedroom.

"Rachel, baby, what are you doing up?" Terra was still half asleep, trying to process everything as she responded.

"Mommy, get up." Rachel repeated. She was standing still in the doorframe, staring in at her exhausted Mother.

"Is everything okay, baby?" Terra asked.

Wait. What was that? Terra thought.

"Mommy, get up." Rachel had said again.

But before that, just before that, Terra could have sworn she heard something else.

Terra glanced around the room. Was that another voice?

"Mommy, I need you to get up." Rachel insisted.

But there it was again, ever so faintly. Terra knew she could hear something. A whisper.

"Rachel, baby, what's going on?" Terra asked her daughter as she sat up in bed.

"Mommy."

Terra felt the back of her neck tingle. The fear raced down to her fingertips and toes. Now she was sure of it. Just before Rachel had spoken, a whisper had called out. A whisper coming from the closet.

Tears were streaming down Terra's cheeks as she looked toward the closet, then back to her daughter.

"Baby, come here. Come here, baby." Terra pleaded with her daughter.

The whisper grew louder, and then Rachel followed.

"Mommy. Get in the closet."

"Wha … what?" Terra responded.

The voice from the closet grew louder still, now a growl. Then Rachel followed again.

"Mommy, get in the closet."

"Rachel, please stop and just come here." Terra begged her daughter as she sobbed.

The voice growled out again, now loud enough for Terra to make out exactly what it said, pulling Terra's eyes to the darkness beyond the closet door. Terra felt her throat tighten to the point of choking.

"Mommy, get in the closet." The vile voice wailed.

Terra looked back to her daughter. *No. Please, no,* she begged internally.

"Mommy," Rachel began. "Get in the closet."

"Stop. Please stop." Terra was barely able to speak through her cries. "Please, Rachel, stop."

"Rachel," the wicked man in the closet began to speak again. "If Mommy won't come in the closet—"

"Leave my daughter alone!" Terra cried. "Leave her alone!"

Insidious laughter echoed from behind the closet's darkness. Then the man continued speaking. "I need you to come in."

Rachel turned toward the closet.

"Rachel, no!" Terra screamed, leaping from her bed. Rachel sprinted toward the closet door. "Stop!" Terra yelled, running to get between her daughter and the closet. "Stop!"

Right as Rachel had reached the closet door, Terra caught her and forcibly threw her back. A quick exhale of relief. Terra was petrified at the thought of what the man in the closet might have done to her.

But she didn't realize. She stopped to exhale, but she was still just outside the doorframe of the closet. Hands quickly jolted from the closet and snatched Terra's hair, pulling her into the darkness.

Screams. Horrid screams and demonic laughter twisted into a nightmarish duet. Terra could see her daughter standing outside the closet, staring in.

"Mommy," Rachel called to her mother. "The man said he'd bring Daddy back home if I did what he said. Mommy, come out now."

But Terra's screams had ceased.

"Mommy?" Rachel called out once more, now in tears and with her voice shaking.

The eyes glared back at Rachel through the veil of darkness before the man spoke. "Come in, Rachel. Mommy and Daddy are waiting for you."

THE SANGUINE PRINCE

Some days, Jared could see cars passing by. His fascination with them kept him occupied for endless hours. It was hard to make out their exact shape for a while. The different models and colors also confused him for some time. Though eventually, he was able to gather that they must come in different sizes and colors but be of the same nature. What a fascinating thought.

He would see them in what appeared to be light speed from his perspective. Peering through a keyhole across an empty room through the tight spaces of a boarded window, and then across the front yard into the street. Mostly they would pass by as streaks of color. But sometimes, sometimes they would stop. Stop long enough to make out the object.

Jared would press his eye against the keyhole so tightly it would tear up. His hands bracing the door, his heartbeat racing, while his breathing grew heavy and cumbersome. He often wondered what these creatures were. But his curiosity would be interrupted by the sound of a door slamming.

By the sound of the door crashing shut that Jared had leaned against for sixteen years, he was able to deduce that there must be more of these devices, connecting other boxes like his, as the same sound his door made when it came shut often came echoing from outside, assumedly from other doors. This noise was a signal to him.

Jared would hear one door slam shut, followed by another; and then his door, one of the four walls of his existence, would burst open. Like having the sky above lifted off by an eons-old deity, staring down in judgment, Jared's reality would be ripped open before his very eyes. Of course, with time, through the shrieks of the nameless man and the stings of the whip he had lashed with, Jared was able to absorb the onslaught and look past it. Only for brief fleeting moments, but in those moments, Jared learned that his four walls were not the only four walls. His reality was not the only reality.

These were the things he would ponder while in the dark, staring at passing cars through a keyhole, across a room, through a window, into a street.

What was life like in other walls? What would life be like without the vile one? The one who lashed? Jared would sometimes have his door opened without being whipped, though. Usually two times a day to receive food and water.

But visits by the nameless man beyond these two were never for anything besides lashings, and scorning. Like all things, though, Jared became used to these encounters. The scar tissue on his skin would open so easily from the lashings that he was virtually always covered in dry blood. Jared's interest in the passing vehicles only became more profound when he realized that some of them had the same color as the liquid he leaked from the lashings.

Fear was a constant, but more than anything, Jared was captured by wonder. Knowing there was more kept his mind busy every day. He could tell he and the nameless man were one and the same, as far as having the same bodies. Arms, legs, things of that nature. Were there more? Or was life outside the window full of the monsters who raced by in different sizes and shapes? Or perhaps those weren't monsters at all but something else entirely. Jared was determined to find out.

For many years, he was small. Jared could tell he had gotten larger, as the walls that housed his existence had only gotten tighter with time. The nameless man was always a towering beast, lashing down with his whip. Whether it was a power he possessed or a tool he crafted, Jared did not know, but between his size and the whip, the idea of fighting back was never contemplated. Only to cower. To cover up. To whimper.

Like all things, survival was the only real intention of Jared. That was burned into his mind the way evolution has done with every creature. Though the new thoughts, the thoughts of seeing what was beyond—those were crafted by Jared himself.

The same way Jared deduced that he and the nameless man were the same, with hair and skin, arms and legs, Jared deduced the man could feel pain. Jared deduced the man could open. Jared deduced that he too could be made to drip this colorful fluid that hardened on his skin. He too could be made red.

The only question was *how*. How would he overcome the power of the nameless man? This gradually led him to experiment: Where could he gouge, strike, grab at his own existence that would inflict pain. Cause discomfort. Draw out the red. So he struck at the leg. Nothing. Not enough to stop anyone anyway. He grabbed at his arm. Not even a slight discomfort. He smacked at his face. Annoying, but nothing like the pain from the lash. He clenched his fist in anger and rammed it down at his groin in another test, but one fueled by rage. He keeled over, whining facedown on the floor. Sickening pain coursed up from his body. Debilitating pain. An unexpected success, he thought to himself as he rocked back and forth on the floor, trying to sooth his anguish. One more place. He would need one more weak spot to attack. Pulling on his fingers, punching at his ribs, smacking on his feet. Where else could he cause as much pain as the first weak spot he had discovered?

Then he placed a finger on his eye and pushed with force. Sickening pain shot through him. He yelped and screamed, his finger lodged into his eye socket, red now streaming down his face. Pure agony, but to the degree of not feeling accomplished in finding a new attack point. Agonizing to the point of forgetting why he had even done it in the first place.

Through his shrieks and the violent pain shooting through his face, Jared didn't hear the two doors slamming shut as he always did before. This time, he saw only his own door wildly swinging open.

The nameless man looked on in horror as Jared stood up screaming, his eye gouged out and smashed lying in the socket, blood pouring out onto the floor.

"Jared, what have you done!" the man hollered in disgust.

The only word Jared knew was Jared. The rest was foreign. The rest was noise. But in this moment of anguish and rage, he acted without thought.

Jared leaped at the man, reaching out for his eyes. The nameless man threw his hands up to shield himself, holding Jared at bay. The two of them swung around, arms intertwined, slamming into the walls of the empty room, until, finally, the man's back came smashing into the far wall by the window. Jared pinned him tightly while still reaching for his eyes.

"Get off me!" the man cried, pushing Jared's arms back.

Jared could tell his first strategy was not working. There was still one more place he knew he could hurt him. Jared quickly yanked his own arm back to free it from the grip of the nameless man, then gripped the man's groin as tightly as he could and pulled and twisted as hard and violently as possible. The man squealed in pain and dropped to his knees. It worked, but before Jared's mind even processed the success of his attack, he released the man's groin and shot both hands into the man's skull, gripping his head and piercing both eyes with his thumbs. The nameless man screamed in agony and brought both hands up to Jared's wrists in an attempt to push them away and free his eye sockets from the puncturing thumbs. It was no use. While his thumbs were still pushing deeper into the skull, Jared turned and slammed the man's head to the floor. The nameless man continued screaming in pain, and Jared matched his screams with cries of rage as he stared down at his tormenter, now oozing the red from both wounds where his eyes once were. Jared stayed there. Jared stayed on top of the motionless body, pushing into the man's eyes with his fingers, striking at his groin, long after the man had stopped screaming or fighting back. Until the red covered the body the way it had always covered Jared.

Jared stood up, still in horrific pain from gouging out his own eye, and peered at the door. Not his door, but the new door. This was the first time he had been anywhere. Like a man arriving on an undiscovered island, or diving into a new unseen depth, Jared was in awe. The pain was still very much there, but it did not matter.

In a full sprint, Jared darted for the door, fumbling with the knob until he was able to maneuver it to open, and then, fear. Jared's sense of wonder was still prominent, but he could not help but be afraid. As the door beyond his door opened, Jared was staring into a whole new existence. With no idea of what to expect, and the size of the world vastly beyond what he'd ever known. What was out there? More men with whips and pain? More men he would have to make red? His fear halted him for a moment longer. Then he stepped out. Traveling around the corridors, Jared was dumbfounded by the structure. Not just four walls. Turns and twists, colors and items. Things he had no idea of their purpose.

Jared's frantic and awe striking tour of the new world was halted when his eye became fixed on a singular object. He couldn't look away. Frozen, amazed, and terrified all at once. A door. A new door. Another new door. If the first led to a new box and the next led to this confusing world of items and objects, what would this third door lead to? He wanted to know, more precisely, he had to know.

He ran to the new door and opened it with cocky pride, almost gloating to himself that he knew how to open them now.

Then he stopped and fell to his hands and knees. What was this? No, no, no. This could not be. Jared pulled all his extremities in tight in a primal display of self-preservation. Looking up and around, panting in horror. What was this place? Blinding rays firing down, loud booming noises as the monsters, which he now knew were indeed monsters, rumbled by. Everything that fascinated him had now become a nightmare. Then one of the monsters stopped.

A passerby slammed her brakes, coming to a screeching halt at the sight of a teenage boy shriveling on the ground naked in front of her neighbor's house, covered in scars and blood.

She quickly threw her door open and ran to him without hesitation to aid the poor boy.

Jared saw the monster flare out its mouth, and from it came another tormentor.

This must be where they come from, he thought.

It shouted noises at him just as the nameless man had, and ran at him frantically. Was this all life was beyond his box? A world of monsters and lashers? Jared knew he could make them stop now, though. He knew if he could make them red, they would stop and leave him alone.

As the woman came within a yard of the trembling young man, she realized his eye was wounded, and still a very fresh wound at that.

"Oh my god, what happened?" she questioned in horror, with her eyes now watering, on the verge of tears at the sight of this tortured boy.

Then before she could react, the boy leaped on her, screaming wildly. She wasn't very large, but even with his malnourished body, he easily overpowered her. She cried out for help, but her cries soon became screams of pain as the boy's fingers pierced both of her eyes. The pressure made her feel as though her head was exploding from the inside, and she quickly realized her calls for help and shrieks of agony were in vain. She knew she would be dead before anyone arrived.

Jared kept pressing down into the lasher's face as hard as he could, now slamming its head into the ground violently over and over as hard as he could with his weak, scarred body. After its screams stopped, Jared pulled his fingers out from the seeping wounds. He knew the nameless lasher was red enough. It would leave him alone now. But his moment of relief was short-lived. As he peered back up, more monsters had stopped. Some ominously lurking. Others, however, opened themselves up, and released more lashers. Many more. Jared wailed and fearfully retreated back into the structure. He wanted it all to be over. He wanted to be back in his box. He wanted it all to end.

Jared sprinted back down the hall and entered the room that housed his box so quickly he lost his balance and fell. The nameless man still lay motionless on the floor, covered in the red. Jared began to wonder, if you made someone red enough, could they ever move again? But no time for thoughts right now. Into his box. Into the only place they couldn't go. He had never seen any other lasher, any other tormentor, until leaving. Jared was sure they could not reach him in here. In the box, he would be safe.

So he entered the door to his existence, and cowered inside, shutting it behind him.

"I'm gonna be sick." Chris was able to muster before gagging, looking down at the mutilated face of the murdered woman.

"Get it together, Chris," Joseph commanded sternly as he walked past the corpse and into the nameless man's house. "Let's get this sicko."

"I'm with you, Joe."

Larry responded, following in pursuit of the scarred killer who mangled the poor woman in cold blood.

Chris reluctantly followed the would-be vigilantes inside, not wanting to be deemed a coward otherwise.

Chris was not at all a small man, but nothing that would alarm you with the threat of an altercation. Joseph and Larry, however, were both above average in height and weight. Joseph, being the biggest of the three men—six feet two and roughly 230 pounds—confidently led the search through the home. Being that the house was not very large, it did not take long to find the room that was all but empty for another eyeless body. And had it not been for the very loud panting and crying coming from the closet, the trio may not have thought to check such a dumbly obvious hiding place.

Jared stayed balled up on the floor of his dark home. He could hear the lashers coming. More than one. His fear was pounding in his chest, and tears streamed out of his remaining eye. He was so sure, or more so, he truly wanted to believe they could not enter his box. He was wrong.

The door flew open, and the first lasher grabbed Jared, ripping him from his sanctuary.

Jared expected lashes. Many, many lashes. This was different. He felt crushing strikes. The pain was different, but still agonizing. His body felt as though it was being pushed into, making it more difficult to breathe with every strike. Jared fell to the floor wheezing, crawling back toward his box.

"No, you don't, you sick freak." Joseph said, pulling at the scarred killer's feet before brutally kicking his bare ribs.

Joseph could feel, and for that matter hear, the ribs of the boy crack. He felt accomplished. He felt justified. He felt heroic.

Jared squealed in pain as he writhed on the floor. These were not lashers. These were crushers. Jared had quickly decided these were worse. Then as the next strike slammed the back of his head, bouncing it off the floor, he felt cracks and splitting pain in his jaw. Barely able to lift his head back up, he could see and feel the red pouring from his mouth, and in that pool of red, he could see teeth scattered about.

"Jesus, Joe, you got him. Chill out, man!"

Chris now pitied the child. He couldn't bear watching him squirm naked and beaten on the floor anymore.

Joseph turned to Chris, glaring with a leaking rage and asked out of spite, "You wanna try and stop me from ending this woman killer? You feel sympathy for people who rip out women's eyes?"

"Nah, Joe, I'm not saying all that. It's just he's done. Look at'm, man."

Jared could hear the noise they spat back and forth at one another. He would have been more curious about what it all meant if it were not for the current predicament. As the question he began to ask himself when he saw the nameless man still motionless, had now reoccurred to him. If you make enough of the red, will you never move again? Jared was so afraid of that idea, and he knew he was covered in it now. How much more could he take? But too many crushers. Too many to make red all at once. So how would he stop them? Then Jared's moment arose. One of the crushers slammed to the floor.

"You can sit down there with him then!"

Joseph had punched Chris clean across the jaw, knocking him unconscious in a single blow, after a short heated exchange. Joseph was in a bloodlust now. He just needed to hurt someone, and this was a wonderful reason to give out hurt. But before he could admire his work for too long, smirking at Chris's sleeping body, Joseph heard the pounding of the scarred killer's feet slamming heavily across the hardwood floor.

"Joe, he's running!" Larry shouted as he took off in pursuit.

Back into the scary world. Back into the unwanted existence. Jared had to act fast. His mind raced and ran through ideas, coming up with them and tossing them out just as fast. Ways to stop the crushers. Then one idea seemed not too irrational to Jared. The lash. The way the nameless man could cause hurt, could open Jared, could make the red. The nameless man could do it very easily with his tool. With the item he always had. What if Jared could find something? An item to make them red faster. He now knew that with enough force, anywhere on him could hurt. So in turn, with enough force, anywhere on them could hurt too. Time was precious now, as the crushers were not far behind, and it wouldn't be long before Jared simply collapsed from his broken ribs. Jared needed to find something quickly. The closest thing in the room of items and objects would have to do. Jared frantically ran toward a raised platform that seemed to have many items. One had a handle, which reminded him of the nameless man's item. It too had a handle. This raised Jared's confidence in his plan. He gripped the handle of the item. It was small and rounded at the end, also heavier than Jared expected. It would have to do. As Jared turned his head, the biggest crusher was within striking distance behind him, closing in.

Joseph was running behind the killer, chasing the beaten boy and fairly impressed with his ability to evade despite his beating. The house was not big, though. Joe knew the murderer could not run for long. As they turned the corner into the kitchen, Joe cornered him. The killer would now receive the rest of his beating. And Joseph intended on making it a death sentence. The only ones here to witness would be Larry and himself. He would kill this psycho.

"Where are you running to, you little sh—"

Joseph's overconfident approach was misguided, as the boy turned unexpectedly and struck him viciously over the head with a frying pan. The top portion of Joseph's skull fractured on impact, and the angle of his fall landed his chin on the marble countertop, forcing his teeth clean through the tongue that was still sticking out.

"Christ!" Larry shouted, watching Joseph twitch on the floor.

That should be enough red, Jared thought, astonished by how much faster this new item could make them stop moving. One more to go.

"Woah, woah, wait!" Larry pleaded with his hands extended, stepping backward out of the kitchen.

Jared wailed out a terrifying war cry as he dashed toward the last of his tormentors. He would make him red. He would make them all red.

"Wait!" Larry tried one last time, but clearly knew it would not be a useful plea as he preemptively turned toward the door and ran.

Jared was so full of adrenaline from his prior success that his body forgot it had broken ribs, but it soon remembered, and he fell to his knees, gripping his sore side. The ache was horrendous. Jared was sure he could take no more. Any more at all and he would never move again. Suddenly a sound caught Jared's attention—moaning outside of his own coming from back in the kitchen.

Joseph had come to. He could barely see; he was badly concussed, the blood flowing from his cranium all but blinding one eye, and the sharp pain in his mouth from his severed tongue. It took Joe a moment to piece together where he was and what happened. Slowly, he was able to get the strength to put his hands on the kitchen floor and push himself to a knee. Still dazed, but seeing a little more clearly now, he raised his head to see the scarred killer standing before him. Looming overhead, his hand raised with the frying pan ready to deliver another blow. Joseph tried crying out pleas for mercy, but his tongue could not allow it from the floor. Cowering, he brought his hands together as if to pray, in an attempt to show his sorrow in a gesture. But Joseph did not know Jared. And Jared did not know God.

Jared saw the crusher on his knees, making grunts and squeals, putting his hands up for what Jared assumed was a lousy defense against his next attack. In that moment, Jared learned a primal instinct. The desire to be the one standing above those who kneel. The desire to make others red, who have made you red. Jared brought the frying pan down onto the crusher's head, the first strike slightly intercepted by hands, but still enough to make the man go flat onto the floor again. Jared decided not to stop. He decided to keep striking his head until the red was everywhere. From the doorway of the house, the third crusher still stood watching in horror.

That was where Jared learned another lesson. Make enough red, and the tormentors will run away.

A Drink of Gems

From a land of skyscrapers,
A traveler arrived,
To the sea of gold sands,
Where Ra rips through the skies.

He intended an adventure,
He wished for a story,
To bring home to his colleagues,
A tale of bold glory.

But the desert was vast,
And the traveler unprepared.
He'd been swallowed by the sea,
In the dry desert air.

Shimmering hills overlapped,
Like rows of curved glass.
The traveler's skin being pelted,
With gusts scraping sand past.

His canteen had a final drop,
It had only been two days.
But water goes quickly,
Underneath the desert sun's rays.

The traveler trudged over dunes,
His sweat began to cease,
The sand began to mock him,
Birds circled for a feast.

When just barely in the distance,
The traveler noticed to his right,

A man stood behind a table,
A strange and curious sight.

But surely this meant salvation,
A man out in the sands,
He must have come from a town close by.
The traveler turned to him and ran.

As the traveler grew closer,
There was more to ponder at.
He saw the man wore robes with jewels,
And his face hid beneath his hat.

He approached the man.
"Hello, hello!"
The traveler joyously greeted.
The man's response was as so.

"I am the merchant,
Amongst the sands.
If you care to trade
Sift through my stand."

The traveler was puzzled
By the response of the merchant.
Surely out here,
He understood this was urgent.

"I'm not here to trade,
I'm close now to death.
I need spare water,
And a place I may rest."

The merchant looked on,
Then the merchant shook his head.
"That is unfortunate, my friend,
For I cannot trade with the dead."

The traveler was appalled.
What a treacherous fiend.
"You'd mock my condition?
The sun will claim me with its gleam."

"No, my friend,"
The merchant said to reassure.
I do not mock you now.
My intentions are pure."

"Then you must help me,"
The traveler began.
"I have nothing to trade,
I cannot meet your demand."

"There is always something,"
The merchant responded with haste.
"I take all forms of payment,
I leave nothing to waste."

On the merchant's table lay silks,
Kettles and crocs' teeth,
Furs and oils,
But water was the traveler's need.

"I just need a drink,
Before the desert claims my life.
I will give you my wallet for your water."
This bargain would end the traveler's strife.

The merchant raised his hand,
But not to take the man's wallet,
Instead to stop the transaction.
He found this proposal appalling.

"Out here in the sand,
My water is worth much more than your money.

Rarer than diamond,
And sweeter than honey."

"It's all that I have,
There is nothing else."
The merchant pointed at once.
"Your ring would work well."

The traveler dismissed this.
"It's an heirloom, unfortunately."
The merchant shrugged,
"Then my water will stay with me."

"Please reconsider!"
The traveler pleaded and cried.
"Perhaps my ring could be yours,
And your water could be mine."

"Excellent, excellent."
Replied the merchant of the sands.
They traded their possessions,
Then the merchant insisted on shaking hands.

The traveler guzzled the water.
The merchant placed his prize on his stand.
Then he turned his back and walked away,
Disappearing into the desert wind.

Once the merchant was gone,
And clear out of vision,
The traveler could not help,
But take some provisions.

Some food and some trinkets,
Most importantly his ring.
To leave it behind,
Would be such a poor thing.

But the traveler's slick thieving,
Would not take him far.
He crossed one dune,
To see the merchant holding a scimitar.

"You knew the deal,
I'd presented the water's wage."
The merchant said, glaring down
With ruby-red rage.

"A priceless gem for your water!
The deal was unfair!"
The traveler cried out,
In horrid despair.

"Items are worth where they are,
And your needs set the price.
When you need a drink in my desert,
Gems won't suffice."

The merchant took back his belongings,
The traveler lost his head.
But before the killing stroke,
The last words that were said:

"Never travel in the desert with more money than water,
Never steal from a man who shakes hands when he barters."

Trinkets, and Things

We had just arrived back at the king's palace. Such a flamboyant manor. Come to think of it, I'd always hated being summoned there. Fat aristocrats. Rich dainty women. All bathing in their mutual love of patrimonial gold and power. The noise throughout the halls was deafening. Every drooling moron boasting of adventures they had never taken, or money they did not earn. *None of these slobs have ever held a blade,* I thought to myself. *None of them have ever worked for a single coin they own. Disgusting. Dishonorable. Filth.* I, of course, kept my dialogue internal, as a single member of this "noble" society hearing me would have meant death. About a dozen other Royal Champions and I had been chosen from the ranks of the thirty-five who had survived the duty given forth by the king, to deliver these gauntlets to his majesty himself.

I had no clue what about these old rusted gloves could have been so important, that seventy of the finest warriors in the kingdom had to be slain by Harbingers to retrieve them. But I would soon find out, I said to myself. We approached the king's throne. The high priest standing, more lurking, by his side. The darkened red robes he wore, accompanied by his long gray hair and loose old skin, left the high priests presence always feeling ominous, at the very least. Then, of course, the king, who I had now seen a number of times during my time as a Royal Champion, sat arrogantly on his throne. His purple robe very purposefully three feet longer than it needed to be and studded with jewels that undoubtedly cost many good soldiers their lives to obtain on his orders. His crown pure gold, and as obnoxious as his other garments.

The long walk up the palace stairs and through the palace's long halls had the other Champions and me breathing heavily, as we were ordered to wear full combat armor when delivering this bounty to our king. Nonsensical customs. Nothing new for us.

"Quiet down now, quiet down." The king demanded as he waved his ornament-covered hand.

The entirety of the Royal Champions stood at attention before the king. Besides myself. I stood upright still, but my hands were holding forth these decrepit gauntlets that the king desired so.

"We owe a great debt to our wonderful, brave, ferocious Royal Champions!" the king exclaimed.

The crowed of wellborns cheered with fake glee, wishing to appease their king. Disgusting cowards. Their delight repulsed me.

"I have been waiting for this moment for what seems like a lifetime now," the king continued as he passed his eyes across us, and then raised them to his mobs. "The moment where I, King Samuel the Fourth, would control all of the Arcreed."

Cheers erupted.

Wait. What? I thought to myself. What is he talking about?

The high priest began shuffling his way down the stairs from the king's throne toward me.

"With the seizure of the final piece of Bathos's armor, we will finally become the one and only kingdom!" the king announced proudly, as he raised his hands amused with his own banter.

Bathos? I continued my dialogue with myself. *Who is Bathos? And what magic did this glove possess that makes you think you can conquer a world?*

I could sense that I was not the only member of the Royal Champions who stood bewildered. The high priest had made his way down the stairs, and stopped in front of me.

"Champion," the priest began with his fizzled out dying voice. "Your sacrifice to acquire this magnificent artifact shall be remembered for all times."

The priest then reached out with his crooked hands and took the gauntlets from me before turning to carry them back up the staircase toward the king.

"My Lord." The crowd gasped. "My Lord, I must object."

The voice came from behind me. A member of the Royal Champions had spoken, and out of place.

"Who dare use their tongue before the king unprovoked!" the old priest hissed, glaring down on us with his foul gaze.

"Relax, old man." The king said, waving off the high priest.

What are you thinking? I questioned to myself. Speaking in the king's palace without an invitation to do so meant death.

"You there," the king scoffed, pointing toward the champion behind me to my left. "You shall be granted speech before me, as I am curious of your intent. But you shall have your throat slashed for your infraction upon the end of our discussion."

"Yes, my king. Of course, my king." Replied the brave champion.

I had seen beasts ten times the size of men ravage countrysides. The dwelling of witches with scattered remains of children. War-torn battlefields soaked in the blood of soldiers from both banners. Harbingers ripping men limb from limb. But for some reason, this champion speaking before the king in his hall shook my very soul.

"Go ahead now, boy." The king's address to the champion enraged me. "What is it you have given your life for to share with us?" The king finished.

The champion stepped out of formation but remained at attention. "My king, you must not awaken Bathos." The Royal Champion calmly stated.

The king looked puzzled.

"Nonsense, my Lord!" the high priest cried. "This boy knows nothing of the ancient gods. Hearing his treasonous tongue sickens me."

The king glanced over at the high priest, then back toward the bold champion, who stood alone. "Would you elaborate on that, champion?" the king mockingly asked.

"Yes, my king," the champion replied. "Bathos will do no deal with you. He is no god. He is a devil."

What were they speaking of? I'd thought to myself once more. I had never heard of any Bathos, and the only ancient gods I'd known were slain by the god Rugor. Or so the story went. But this Bathos, I'd never heard of him. Nor did I have any clue what these old gloves we had raided a cave of Harbingers for had to do with it.

"Silence. Enough from you. Champions, cut his throat." The king said passively as he waved his hands toward the outspoken champion.

I stood completely still. I could not slay this man, but I prayed another one among my ranks would do so quickly to prevent our entire group from being slaughtered for treason. No more than a moment later, I could hear the gashing of the champion's throat and his final gasps for air as his body struck the floor. I could not see him die, as I was now standing at attention, facing toward the king, as was custom. I am forever thankful I did not watch that heroic Champion die so dishonorably.

"Any other thoughts on the matter?" the king asked, seeming to be serious, as though he truly expected another poor soul to speak up.

"My Lord," the high priest said as he lowered the gauntlets to the king's feet. "You now have every piece of Bathos's armor. We merely need to assemble them to call him forth."

"Wonderful, wonderful!" the king cheered, with a childlike grin smeared across his face.

The Royal Guard marched out from behind the king's private halls, carrying separate pieces of armor. My eyes shot back and forth, attempting to examine each individual piece.

Helmet ... , I said to myself. *Cuirass ... greaves...*

I had no doubt the old armor the guard was carrying was part of the same set that the gauntlets we had captured did. What was going on? The guard placed the armor pieces at the bottom of the stairs, just a few feet in front of where I stood. One of them climbed the staircase and stood before the king. He bowed, then reached down to retrieve the gauntlets from the floor before the king's feet. The high priest tottered his way back down the stairs towards me to begin assembling the armor on the ground. He laid each piece of armor out accordingly, placing the helmet above the Cuirass, which had been placed on its back, with the greaves beneath it. Finally, the gauntlets were placed on each respective side of the cuirass. What strange sorcery was this old man attempting here? The king looked on pleasantly, awaiting his prize.

"My wonderful servants, with the acquisition of all the pieces of Bathos's armor, we will now call him forth and negotiate for his allegiance to our kingdom!" the king pronounced.

Madman! What sort of insane story did this priest tell you? I had to contain my outburst to not suffer the same fate as the last Champion who spoke out of turn.

The high priest raised his hands and lowered himself to his knees. "Behold. Bathos." I looked down at him. *What a fool,* I said to myself. *What an absolute ...* Then I saw for myself. The armor. It was moving. Black mist materialized within the steel, and the armor began to shake violently. A loud piercing screech ripped through the air as the mist began to thicken within the plates. The crowd of nobles gasped and whispered among themselves. The armor began to rise into the air, forming into the shape of a man. The king's eyes widened, and his juvenile smile remained painted on his face. Though he remained seated before what he thought was going to be a god forming before him. Foolishly arrogant, or perhaps ignorant, or perhaps both. Black mist swirled violently around the armor, and through it, I could see what was taking shape. No longer was I looking at empty plates. The armor was filled. I was standing before a massive being. His armor no longer looked old and brittle but a potent black, devoid of all scars and blemishes. The helmet's cover was down, shielding the face of the entity before me. The mist slowly dissipated until there was no more. All that was left was a massive imposing presence towering over us.

"Bathos!" the king called out joyously. "It's a pleasure to have you in my palace at last!"

"Who," the deep tormenting rasp of this being's harrowing voice rived through our ears as it spoke. "Who brought me here?"

The large figure peered around the room, then looked straight down toward me, trapping my soul. I was then set free as he turned his attention toward the king, who had begun to answer the fiend.

"I did, Bathos. I, King Samuel the Fourth, have brought you before me, to make a deal."

The king still seemed confident. As if he still believed he had control of everything. But I already knew something was not right. I had been stared down by countless creatures and monsters. But nothing before had ever made my heart sink as this being did, by simply looking toward me. Something about him was wrong.

The high priest looked up toward the black-armored figure in awe. "Bathos, the great god of exchange, we have called you here for …"

"Silence!" the king roared, glaring down from his throne at the high priest. "I will speak for myself before this god."

The king's demeanor went from scolding to endearing as he turned his attention back toward his summoned would-be benefactor.

"Bathos, I have brought you here to make an exchange. I have gathered your armor to summon you before me so that you may help me in my conquest of the world. In exchange, I shall provide you with all the riches and slaves you could ever desire!" the king gleefully exclaimed to the silent being.

The dark god tilted his head and looked back over top of me into the crowd of wellborns.

"Trinkets, and things." The beast whispered, slowly turning his gaze back toward the king. "Trinkets, and things." It said again.

"I'm sorry?" the king replied, leaning forward from his throne, as if he may have misheard something.

"You brought me here. To offer trinkets, and things." The ghastly voice murmured.

"Well, not exact … ," the king tried to respond.

"You offer me trinkets, and things." The monstrosity interrupted. "I, Bathos, the god of exchange, have been brought forth to barter with a mortal offering trinkets, and things."

The massive figure took a step up the stairs toward the king, with the Royal Guard standing by to provide the king the illusion of protection.

"You misunderstand!" the king blurted confidently. "I have the most vast wealth this world has ever seen, and you will be rewarded with anything you could possibly desire!"

The king's demeanor still seemed uplifted. So clearly spoiled all his life that he had no concept of not being in control.

"Yes," Bathos began, his voice still chilling to the very foundation of my being. "You seek my help in exchange for trinkets, and things."

Bathos took another step, getting closer again to the sitting king.

"I am eternal, you insignificant waste," Bathos howled at the king. "I have no mundane desires." Bathos continued toward the king; the Royal Guard remained in position.

"Surely, there is something I can offer you?" the king said in a fragile voice.

The devil stopped his approach toward the king. "You wish to bargain? I seek agony."

"Agony?" the king started. "Agony of whom?"

The fiend glared at the king, piercing through his facade of confidence. "The agony of ten thousand souls." Bathos stated.

"Ten thousand?" the king asked in despair.

"Ten thousand," Bathos repeated. "You wish to bargain with me, mortal? With your trinkets, and things? You will give me the pain and anguish of ten thousand souls by the time the next night falls. Or I shall exact that payment upon you. This is my bargain."

"Wait, I ... ," the king began to cry out.

"You have until nightfall. I will receive my suffering from ten thousand souls, or I shall inflict the pain of ten thousand souls being torn apart on you." Bathos turned away from the king and walked back down the staircase toward me. "You may keep your trinkets, and things."

"Bathos, please reconsider my offer!" the king shrieked as he hurled himself up from his throne.

A black mist ripped through the air once more, and just as quickly as he'd arrived, Bathos disappeared, and the black mist faded. He was gone, leaving the king in horror. I don't know how many peasants the king had massacred that day. Children, infants, women. No one was spared. He even started having the nobles executed toward the end of the day. But however many it was, it must not have been ten thousand.

WHO WOKE TO THE VOID

Cold … so cold … , I thought as I awoke, lying on my back in the middle of a field covered in a light blanket of snow. I looked at my hands: red and numb from resting in the snowy pasture.

How did I get here? What's going on? I asked myself as I searched my surroundings, the stale night air gripping my throat with each breath I took. As I looked around, I saw that the meadow I'd woken up in was shared by four goats, three of which were wandering aimlessly. But one, one was locked onto me. His fur was a matte black, and his stagnant gaze was troubling me. The small goat stood a few meters before me.

Where the hell am I? I questioned to myself once more. The shrieks of the frozen wind howled in my ears as its sharp gusts whipped across my skin. I postured up and folded my arms across my chest, in a vain attempt to shelter myself from the cold. At the edge of the field I had woken up in was a wood edge, consisting of tall, swaying trees. The forest was thick, and dark. The full moon overhead was the only source of light, which was faintly descending onto the murky night.

The sound of snow shifting jolted me. I quickly aimed my sight back toward the goats. They had all turned toward the forest. I peered back toward the woods, where a shadow caught my eye. It stepped forward out of the darkness. The moonlight revealed a woman. She was still too far away for me to make out any features, but her presence was chilling.

What is she doing out here alone? In the woods of all places? I called out to her. "Hello?" No response. She was far enough away that I did not feel an immediate threat, but her silence only added to my unease.

I could see her starting to move, her arms reaching out to me, almost welcoming, though the figure remained mute.

"Hello?" I yelled out one more time, this attempt louder than the last, trying to project over the foul gusts of frozen wind. She began moving toward me. Not running, but striding directly toward me at a steady pace. My throat tightened up, and my heart plummeted into my stomach. I bounced to my feet and raced in the other direction. I still had no clue where I was or what was happening. Nor did I know who this woman was, and I was not eager to find out. As I ran, my feet crunched through the snow, and thoughts ricocheted through my head. Where was I running to? I came to a small wooden fence. I quickly climbed over it and kept dashing away from the mysterious woman from the woods. Horrible thoughts began manifesting in my mind, thoughts about what she would do to me, if she caught me. The horrific pictures faded from me as I stumbled upon a road. I'm saved, I said to myself as I turned directions and began running along the blacktop. Surely, this road will lead to someone. Anyone, anyone who could tell me where I was. Anyone but that woman in the woods.

As I continued along the road, the wood line got closer and closer, finally meeting the road's edge on both sides. The treetops blotted out nearly all the light cast from the gleaming moon, leaving me in darkness. My breathing became labored, as I feared what may be lurking just a few steps away from me, lurking in the woods. The skin on my neck felt tight, and each movement I made was strained, I felt eyes on me, prowling from the forest. Suddenly, a light in the distance. What appeared to be a house. I hoped. I was relieved, and my horror slowly melted into comfort at the thought of finding refuge. While I trudged through the snowy road, the light got closer and closer.

Yes! I cried internally, It is a house. I smiled and continued toward the sanctuary. My cheerfulness quickly washed away, and my smile faded as I felt a viscous chill ripping down my spine. I could almost physically feel a presence behind me. I stopped in the road to glance over my shoulder. She stood dormant in the middle of the road, again not too close to feel immediate danger. But still much closer than she had been before. Her passive skulk violently shifted into a crazed dash toward me. I cried out in terror and turned back toward the house in a sprint. I could hear her. The snow crunching, and her feet pounding against the ground, getting closer and closer. My legs felt unstable and weak, like they could give out at any moment. Sweat exuded from my face. I quickly glanced over my shoulder, still running for my life. The woman had almost caught up to me. Her dark hair thrashed back and forth while her arms flailed wildly, as if she were rabid. Looking back was a mistake. After I'd seen her horrific posture chasing me down, my skin raised up even more, horrified at the thought of what would happen when she caught me. She continued to get closer and I could begin to hear her breathing. It was harsh and unmeasured. She began wailing loudly and the sound of her feet thudding against the snowy blacktop was now right behind me. If I can just make it to the house, I'd thought. It's right there. Right there. Just a few more meters. Then, the wailing stopped. I kept running, of course. I reached the driveway of the desolate home, then finally stopped running, gasping for air. I scanned around me. Nothing. She was gone. My deep breaths welcomed the brisk air into my lungs, not minding the cold at all, after what I'd just escaped. I was simply happy to have gotten away from that woman. My hands gripped my knees, and I bent over at the waist, still sucking in air relentlessly. I looked up the short driveway at the two-story home. Lights shone brightly through the windows, comforting me. I was finally relaxed. I walked up the driveway toward the front porch. I then climbed the small staircase and extended a hand to knock firmly, but politely, on the door.

I waited eagerly for an answer, while still peering cautiously over my shoulder, hoping not to see that woman hiding in the dark.

While I was looking into the black night, I heard the door open. I quickly shifted my attention back toward the door. A tall, well-groomed man stood before me. His presence felt somewhat warming. He was clean shaven, and his hair was short and dark. I was off put, as he was wearing a suit and tie. But that was the least of my concerns, given the situation.

"Hello, sir" I started "I'm so sorry to bother you tonight, but someone was chasing me and this was the only place I could run to." I was praying he wouldn't turn me away. I had no other hope.

"Oh my goodness," the man responded with a gasp. "Someone was chasing you?" He looked concerned. He reached out and put his hand on my shoulder and led me inside. "Come in, it's freezing outside." the man exclaimed.

I felt my body loosen and all the stress wash away as I stepped into the warm, calm home. "Thank you, sir. Thank you so much," I praised the tall gentleman for his assistance.

The man began walking toward a large wooden table in what appeared to be a comfortable and quaint dining room.

"Please, take a seat." he said as he pulled out a chair at the table for me.

I continued toward the dining room and sat at the chair the man had offered. He then walked around to the other end of the long wooden table and sat facing me. I let out a long sigh of relief.

"What were you doing out there?" the man asked.

I looked around the room aimlessly, still recovering from the events I'd just experienced.

"Hello?" the man said, trying to get my attention.

I snapped out of it. "I'm sorry. I ... I don't know." I answered.

"You don't know?" the man responded curiously.

I paused before answering. "No. No, I don't." I had finally caught my breath after fleeing from the woman on the road. "I just woke up in a field not too far from here. There were goats. And ... and a woman."

"A woman?" the man asked.

"Yes, a woman." I answered.

"Is that who was chasing you?" he continued.

"Yes. Yes, she was chasing me down the road." I tilted my head down and rested my face on my hands, wondering whether I would be rude to ask about using his phone.

Then the man spoke again. "I'm happy she came down from the woods."

What? I thought. I slowly raised my face from my palms and looked back toward the man.

"I didn't say she came out of the woods." I said back to him. His uncanny knowledge made me wary.

"You didn't have to," the man began. "It's all forest here. You leave here, and it's all the same." His statement was puzzling to me. "What do you mean it's all the same?"

"This place." The man's eyes began to dim. "It's all the same."

"I … I should go." I said to the man. I began to feel uneasy.

"It's okay," the man exclaimed, smiling at me. "It's all the same here. You might as well be the same. For you, for her. For us."

"What are you talking about?" I asked. The light in the room became dull. Slowly closing in around the table.

The man continued to smile. His eyes were now entirely black. "Do it for you. Do it for her. Do it for us."

He then reached down and pulled a handgun out from under the table. He placed it on the tabletop.

"Please," I begged with a whimper. "Please just let me go."

A tear rolled down my face. I couldn't handle all that had unfolded in the past hour.

"Go?" The man's voice began to distort and crack. "There is nowhere. Nowhere to go." He then slid the pistol across the table toward me.

"Do it for you. Do it for her. Do it for us." he said once more.

Whispers. Whispers were creeping up from behind me. Out from the blackness of the room surrounding us, the woman from the woods appeared behind me. Looming over me. I leaped out of my chair and raced for the door. I gripped the doorknob and whipped the door open. There in front of me stood the suited tall man. His eyes were black and piercing. He reached out, holding the gun.

"Do it for you. Do it for her. Do it for us." the man repeated while trying to give me the gun. I looked to the floor, now with tears flowing from my face. I took the gun, examining the weapon, still wondering why I was here. As I raised my head, I pointed the gun toward the tall man. My ears rang, and I closed my eyes as I felt blood splatter across my face. I threw the gun down. The man's body lay lifeless on the floor. I had killed him.

Walking. So much walking. I'll find something. Someone. Eventually. The long dark road seemed endless. My face was still covered with blood while the frigid air aggravated my skin. I held my head low as I wondered, my feet growing more numb with each step. Step after step after step. Then suddenly, I stopped. My eyes peered up in front of me. The tall man was standing there. He smiled and then reached out, offering the gun to me. "Do it for you," he said again. "Do it for her." I reached my hand out to accept the gun. "Do it for us." he finished.

I jolted awake. Where? Where am I now? It was not cold anymore. But still snowing, still in the dark. I stood up. I was in the forest. I circled around, trying to grasp my surroundings. On one side of me was a thick, seemingly endless forest. On the other was the wood's edge. I walked toward the opening of the forest. I stood at the edge of the woods, and peered down into a field. I saw a lone man, lying out in the snow-covered grass. He slowly rose to his feet. The man appeared to be distressed. But finally. Finally I wasn't alone.

I reached out to the man, welcoming him.

WINDOWS

A man with one eye,

For he used the other to bargain.

When God ignored his prayers,

Seeming intent to starve him.

He called to the Devil,

And to his astonishment,

The Devil appeared at once,

To bestow his allotment.

At first the man was afraid,

But the Devil assured him,

He was simply here to make a deal,

For the man's call had lured him.

"I can give to you riches,

You will be free of your impoverished past,

And just two simple things from you

Is all that I ask."

The Devil's offer elated the man,

Finally, his wishes coming true,

But what two things could the Devil want?

"What is it I can offer you?"

The Devil responded with a grin.

"The eyes are windows to the soul, you see,

And you were born with two,

Why not give one to me?"

"Yes, oh yes!" the man shouted with glee.

"That is the first price, what else do you need?"

The Devil told the man, that to his relief,

"The second is simple, abolish your creed."

The man cheered and laughed

As he pulled his eye from its socket,

Then denounced his God

To fill up his pockets.

Treasures he'd dreamed of, his wealth would abound.

He thanked the Devil as he waved him goodbye.

For years the man prospered,

For years he would go on sprees,

Tossing his wealth at all his one eye could see.

But after many long years, he began to notice an error.

His wealth was vast, but not infinite, he realized in terror.

"Please! Devil, please! Return unto me!

I have another eye, if that's what you need."

After all this time of living a life so carefree,

The man could not imagine going back to poverty.

Once more, through flames, the Devil appeared.

"Hello, my dear friend, it's been a few years."

The Devil took the man's eye and left him with gold.

"Make this money last until you grow old."

The man cheered and laughed, the Devil saving him once more.

He'd cursed his God, now the Devil he adored.

For seven days he prospered,

Seven days he bathed in bills,

But on the eighth day the man had grown deathly ill.

No doctor could tell him what was going wrong,

No healer could save him,

His final hour would not be long.

"Devil! Oh Devil! I need you again!

Not for riches now, but instead for medicine."

Now, as before, the Devil came to the man.

The man sighed with relief at the sound of Satan.

"It seems you are dying. A cure holds a heavy price."

"Anything! Anything!" the man cried back to him twice.

"I'll restore your body.

You will be brand new,

you'll live until the old age

of one hundred and two."

"Thank you! Thank you!" the man had begun.

"So what do you need in return this time my old friend?"

"I've peered through both windows,

And liked what I saw.

Your soul will be payment,

When I next come to call."

The man cried in horror,

"Please no, there must be something else!"

The Devil shook his head at the blind man, and welcomed him to hell.

The Devil grinned and sang,

"A deal is a deal."

The man begged and he pleaded, but to no avail.

Blind with riches, health with no soul.

A good man can be tricked into everything, and nothing at all.

LEVIATHAN

"Dr. Timms, right this way."

Dr. Timms had never seen a room so cluttered while also seeming that everyone understood their way through the chaos.

"Dr. Timms, this is Mr. Franklin, NASA administrator."

The short-haired blonde woman who had led Dr. Timms inside then vanished through the mob of frenzied NASA employees.

It was hard to focus. Timms's eyes scoured the room. Bright lights shining down on the crowd of scurrying workers. The sounds of radio chatter and each individual in the room compiling over one another became a blur. Desks with more buttons and screens, flashing lights, and monitors.

Eight? he spoke to himself internally. No, twelve.

He couldn't keep counting before Mr. Franklin's greeting interrupted his thought.

"Dr. Timms," he started, "great to have you here."

The doctor seemed puzzled, as the tall broad-shouldered man, looking older and mature, reached out to shake his hand. He was wearing a suit that undoubtedly cost more than anything he owned. The young doctor was visibly intimidated.

"Thank you, Mr. Franklin, it's nice to meet you." Dr. Timms responded, in an almost uncertain voice. "If you don't mind me asking," Timms continued, "um ... why exactly am I here?" Franklin turned and began walking, his demeanor clearly demanding Dr. Timms to follow.

"Well, Doctor, we figured you might be wondering that," Mr. Franklin announced as he continued leading the way. "We have experienced an anomaly, and after doing our best to find someone who can explain it, we landed on you."

"Uhh," Dr. Timms stuttered. "Well, Mr. Franklin, I really appreciate that. But I'm ... I'm a marine biologist. What does NASA possibly need from me?"

Mr. Franklin approached a monitor, which appeared to have some sort of sonar and radios attached to the counter beneath it.

"We heard something," Mr. Franklin stated as he turned toward the doctor.

Dr. Timms paused a moment, his eyebrows clearly conveying his confusion. "What? Like ..." The doctor took another pause. "Like from space?"

"That's correct, Doctor." Mr. Franklin replied in a stern tone.

"But that's impossible!" Dr. Timms immediately fired back. "There's no sound in space. There's nothing for sound waves to travel through, it's empty space!"

Mr. Franklin sighed and looked toward the sonar screen, then back toward Dr. Timms.

"Well, Doctor, that is not news to us. But what might be news to you is through the use of gravitational waves, we can hear in space."

Dr. Timms looked toward the Sonar, then back to Mr. Franklin.

"And you think a marine biologist can help, how? Exactly?" The doctor sounded almost worried, if not a bit helpless.

As Dr. Timms looked over his shoulder, he noticed the cluttered room of papers flying and employees frantically pacing began to calm down, and eyes began focusing on him.

"Dr. Timms." Mr. Franklin began. "Please listen to this."

Mr. Franklin reached down to the panel on the desk, pressing his finger on a small yellow button.

An uncanny sinking fell into the doctor's stomach, and the back of his neck began to sweat and his spine shivered.

"That? You heard that from space?" Timms stuttered as he listened to the audio recording. A deep, long echo. Pausing. Then echoing out again, followed by small distinct chirps. The bellow gripped the doctor's heart, and it's horrid rumble made Timm's uneasy to his core. The thought of this sound coming from something, something alive in deep space, harrowed the doctor. Mr. Franklin clicked the yellow button once more, stopping the recording.

"That's correct." Franklin exclaimed as he folded his arms, glancing back up at Dr. Timms. "We compared it to known sounds we have on our own planet, and it most closely resembled that of a whale. Do you concur, Doctor?"

Dr. Timms looked to the floor, his hands growing clammy and the shiver in his spine reaching up to his neck. "Yes. Well, no." He continued. "It doesn't remind me of a whale. It reminds me more of an orca."

"Like a killer whale?" Franklin responded quickly.

"Exactly." Dr. Timms replied as he looked back up from the floor, timidly looking at Mr. Franklin.

"Please, Dr. Timms, just relax. There's absolutely no pressure on you here. We simply thought you could give us some information." Mr. Franklin said, clearly able to see the doctor's distress. The room was completely silent now, besides the conversation between the marine biologist and NASA administrator. Dr. Timms looked over his shoulder once more, feeling the overwhelming weight of the eyes locked on him and the pressure of each ear in the room listening to his every word.

"These, gravitational waves—how big would something have to be to make a sound that loud using these waves?" Timms asked.

"Absolutely massive, we're presuming," Franklin replied. "Possibly something as large as our sun."

The doctor raised one hand to his cheek, scratching his face and wiping the sweat from his forehead.

"Now we're not entirely sure if the waves we responded with are nearly loud enough."

"You what?" Dr. Timms said, interrupting Mr. Franklin, bordering on a scream.

"We tried communicating, but we aren't sure if it will hear anything through the gravitational waves. You see, these waves can be extremely weak," Dr. Timms shouted out, clearly before Mr. Franklin had finished his thought.

"How long ago was this? When did you do that?"

Mr. Franklin unfolded his arms and took a half step back, responding, "Well, it took us a few days to find out who would be best suited to help identify the sound. Then a few days to contact and get you here. So I'm not sure. About, four or five days ago?"

"As big as our sun ... " Timms whimpered.

"Maybe bigger. We don't know." Franklin said in response. The room was cold, and the air began to feel stale as the employees listening in began to contract Dr. Timm's dread, without knowing why. "Doctor, do you mind telling me what's going on here? What am I missing?"

"It called out searching," Timms stated. "And you answered it."

"Yes, we did. Is that a problem?" Franklin questioned.

"Potentially. Potentially, yes. A very, very big problem."

The NASA employees began whispering to one another after hearing Dr. Timms response. Mr. Franklin glared toward the crowd of unnerved workers, silencing their bickering.

"Well, Doctor, it's a whale. Don't whales call to each other?" Mr. Franklin asked, seemingly unconcerned.

Dr. Timms leaned over, resting his hands on the countertop. "No," he responded coldly. "No, it's not like a whale."

"But you said—," Franklin began before being cut off.

"I said it reminded me of an orca." Timms stated as he took his hands off the desk, rising back up to meet Mr. Franklin's eyes.

"What are you telling me here son." Mr. Franklin said commandingly. Dr. Timms bowed his head and nervously ran his fingers through his hair. Then glanced back up.

"Orcas are predators. They aren't always calling out to find other orcas." Everyone in the room silently waited. Curious, but chilled by the doctor's tone. "They use echolocation. Whatever sounds bounce back give the orca an idea of what it's found." Mr. Franklin was now looking concerned too.

"Doctor, what does that mean?" Franklin asked. Dr. Timms looked up to the sonar on the monitor.

"It means something big, presumably the size of our sun, is calling out from deep space to find something to eat," Dr. Timms said softly, his voice shaking. "And you called back to it."

THE CORNER

I could swear the shadow in the corner of my bedroom moved. A subtle shift of darkness I could barely notice from my peripheral vision. It was late, and I'm so exhausted. I know that I am, as I always have, as everyone always does, just playing tricks on myself. Nothing is in the corner of my bedroom. Such a childlike notion that simply because the lights are out, malicious forces are lurking.

Still, the looming fear of a silent onlooker in my bedroom in the later hours of the night makes me tighten my grip on the sheets as though the thin layer of cloth is a bronze shield protecting me from malevolent forces. I know my feet are underneath the covers, but I feel around with my toes and double-check to ensure that they are tightly tucked beneath my futile fortress.

The tingle of fear down my back and up through my arms reminds me that you're never too old to be afraid of the dark. But there it is again. It looks like the outline of a hunched-over man. Standing. Swaying. He's in the corner just watching me try to sleep. The idea itself is enough to lead my brain down a path of anxiety and grimmer thoughts. What would he be doing? A man in the corner of my room. What would his intentions be? To watch? To wait till I'm asleep to come closer and reveal his violent agenda? Ripping and gashing at my throat with the long bony fingers my thoughts have conjured up.

For a moment, I even consider getting up to turn the lights on and save my heart the extra beats until I can calm back down.

No. I'm too old for that. Too old for silly childlike phobias of boogeymen. I know he's not really there. Paranoia is potent. I know he's not really there. Until he laughed.

ONLY THE UNKNOWN

In the darker corners
Of some brighter days,
Where the shadows dance
And the imagination plays,

Tall men watch,
Vile women stare.
Rancor is felt.
Putrid flesh in the air.

Grotesque images wait,
Where nothing takes place.
The veil of blackness reigns,
For these horrors it creates.

You don't fear water,
But the murky depths differ.
You don't fear a man,
But a mask makes you shiver.

Your home is a haven,
Except in the night's prevalence,
When your own long hallways,
Stare back with malevolence.

Those closest to your heart,
Have only happy songs sung.
Though you would spiral in despair,
If they greeted you in tongues.

The call from no one,
That is leaking in your head.

The horrors of a watcher,
You've created with your dread.

It's not the idea,
For when the concept is clear,
You will not be shaken,
Only the unknown you fear.

EVIL HOUSE

Into the Evil House,
My brother had tread.
I watched him from my dreams,
Those dreams I so dread.

The house itself alive,
Walls full of veins.
In the basement dwelt its master,
The Despot of Pain.

He stood taller than a man,
He wore a helm to hide his gaze.
His torso he left bare,
Where his skin was linked with chains.

The chains dragged behind the Despot,
His walk joined by chiming metal.
Hearts linked at the polar ends,
Still beating to warn of peril.

I could hear the chant so plainly,
The house's wicked voice repeated proudly.
The chant echoed in my head.
I could hear it all around me.

"Evil House, Evil House,
There's no escape from Evil House."

With each step my brother took,
The house whispered to its master.
Opening doors to lead my brother,
To the Despot's corrupt rapture.

When I awoke, forces pulled me back,
To see my brother's fate.
Unable to move or cry out,
Forced to witness acts depraved.

The pain took hold of him,
Contorting my brother's flesh.
The House sprouted vessels,
They plunged into his chest.

He cried and writhed,
The Despot tearing away at his anatomy.
When I finally arose from this madness,
My mind sank into calamity.

My brother was fine,
But Evil House's toll was still paid.
For I travel back to that place,
Every night when I lay.

Printed in the USA
CPSIA information can be obtained
at www.ICGtesting.com
LVHW040917230923
759033LV00003B/46

9 798888 107812